Jason waited.

A couple of hours, [a] glance at his watch confirmed [it, made it in ten] minutes under. He made a conscious effort to relax coiled shoulder muscles. He waited and wondered.

Wondered if she would walk right in. Or would she ring the bell, as timid as ever on the surface at least? Would she still have the nerve to look at him with big limpid eyes?

He asked himself again how he could have ever been fooled by such sweet innocence.

She walked right in. She stood in the open doorway and stared at him.

Jason stared right back through narrowed grey eyes, unable to release the arrogance of her glittering golden gaze—unable to believe what he was actually seeing.

Diana Hamilton is a true romantic and fell in love with her husband at first sight. They still live in the fairytale Tudor house where they raised their three children. Now the idyll is shared with eight rescued cats and a puppy. But, despite an often chaotic lifestyle, ever since she learned to read and write Diana has had her nose in a book—either reading or writing one—and plans to go on doing just that for a very long time to come.

Recent titles by the same author:

THE BRIDE WORE SCARLET
THE UNEXPECTED BABY

MISTRESS FOR A NIGHT

BY
DIANA HAMILTON

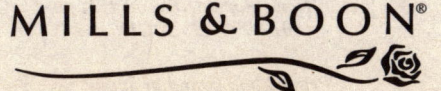

DID YOU PURCHASE THIS BOOK WITHOUT A COVER?

If you did, you should be aware it is **stolen property** as it was reported *unsold and destroyed* by a retailer. Neither the author nor the publisher has received any payment for this book.

All the characters in this book have no existence outside the imagination of the author, and have no relation whatsoever to anyone bearing the same name or names. They are not even distantly inspired by any individual known or unknown to the author, and all the incidents are pure invention.

All Rights Reserved including the right of reproduction in whole or in part in any form. This edition is published by arrangement with Harlequin Enterprises II B.V. The text of this publication or any part thereof may not be reproduced or transmitted in any form or by any means, electronic or mechanical, including photocopying, recording, storage in an information retrieval system, or otherwise, without the written permission of the publisher.

This book is sold subject to the condition that it shall not, by way of trade or otherwise, be lent, resold, hired out or otherwise circulated without the prior consent of the publisher in any form of binding or cover other than that in which it is published and without a similar condition including this condition being imposed on the subsequent purchaser.

MILLS & BOON and MILLS & BOON with the Rose Device are registered trademarks of the publisher.

*First published in Great Britain 1999
Harlequin Mills & Boon Limited,
Eton House, 18-24 Paradise Road, Richmond, Surrey TW9 1SR*

© Diana Hamilton 1999

ISBN 0 263 81746 6

*Set in Times Roman 10½ on 12¾ pt.
01-9908-43515 C1*

*Printed and bound in Spain
by Litografia Rosés, S.A., Barcelona*

CHAPTER ONE

JASON HARCOURT'S right hand hovered over the telephone for a second, then dropped down to his side. He pushed both hands into the side pockets of his dark, well-worn cords and hunched his wide shoulders.

The room was crowding in on him. The over-ornate French antiques, the baroque-framed paintings, the fussy carpets suffocating him. He paced to the long, elaborately draped French windows, dark brows drawn down over flint-grey eyes as he stared moodily out over Lytham Court's winter-bleak gardens.

How he hated this place!

Seven years since he'd set foot over the doorstep—except for the hour he'd spent here after Harold's second wife Vivienne's funeral—and he was only here now because he had no real option. Lytham held bad memories, more than a few.

Following Vivienne's death, four years ago, he had made peace, of a sort, with Harold, the man who had legally adopted him almost thirty years ago on his marriage to Jason's widowed mother. For a three-year-old child, whose real father had been killed in a climbing accident before he was born, it had been easy enough to accept the substitute.

Only after his mother had died of leukaemia, when he was seventeen, had he begun to see his adoptive father with new eyes.

But that was in the past, and the tentative peace had progressed relatively smoothly because he had stipulated that their occasional meetings took place at the older man's London club. Neutral ground. He was glad, now, that he'd gone with the flow, somewhat sceptically giving Harold the benefit of the doubt when he had insisted he'd changed. He owed his adoptive father that much.

But the scepticism had hardened to downright disbelief when at their last meeting, two months ago, Harold had told him, 'Georgia's been back in England for six months now; we've been meeting fairly regularly.'

Jason had watched the way the mere mention of her name had made Harold's tired, faded eyes brighten in the older man's face, a face that had shrunk in on its own bones. Harold had gone downhill, slowly but very surely, since Vivienne had died, and his obvious physical frailty had been the only thing that had stopped Jason from getting up from the lunch table and walking out of the muted dark brown atmosphere of the club and into the relative sanity of London's teeming streets.

'So you keep in touch with Georgia.' He practically spat the words out, the old bitterness surfacing as it always did whenever he was unguarded enough to think about her.

'Since Vivvie died, yes. She, God rest and bless

her, was the stumbling block there. Wouldn't have her daughter's name mentioned.' Harold pushed his barely touched meal aside. Jason speared a forkful of game pie with smooth savagery, debated whether he wanted it, decided not, and laid down his cutlery.

'I know you said you were going to break the long silence and phone New York to tell her of Vivienne's death,' he said carefully. He had offered to put his personal distaste aside and break the news of the fatal car accident, to spare Harold, but the old man had insisted he was the one to do it. As it turned out no one need have bothered; she hadn't cared enough to attend her own mother's funeral.

'Well, yes.' Old eyes fell uneasily. 'There were things that had to be said, and I said them,' he stated enigmatically. 'And I like to think we got close again after the air was cleared. It doesn't do to hold on to old grudges. In any case, she's well settled back in England now. She heads up one of the design teams at the branch of her advertising agency in Birmingham—you'll remember she went out with the girl Sue's family when the father opened a branch in New York?'

Jason glanced fiercely at his watch. He'd had enough of this. Of course he remembered!

'I thought we might all get together at Lytham one weekend soon,' Harold said. 'Mend fences. You and little Georgia are the only family I have left.'

'Spare me the sentimentality.' Jason flung his napkin down. 'It's not impressing me.' He stood up.

'It was worth a try.' The faded eyes held a sudden

gleam of humour. 'But you will come? I'll fix a weekend with Georgia. Be like old times.'

Old times he could do without. 'In your dreams!' he said, and walked out.

He hadn't seen Harold since. He'd meant to, of course he had, but work had got in the way. He regretted that now that Harold was dead, he thought, his eyes still fixed on the dreary garden scene.

It was raining now, icy needles that clattered against the window pane, and the short winter day was ending. The housekeeper, Mrs Moody, had told him that a hard frost was forecast for tonight.

It meant driving conditions would be tricky in the morning. Georgia would probably decide not to risk the icy roads. She hadn't bothered to grab a flight and get over for her mother's funeral, so why should she put herself out to attend Harold's?

Unless she wasn't totally sure of the way her stepfather had left his money and was anxious to find out, he thought cynically.

His hard mouth pulled down, he strode over to the phone and lifted the receiver.

Georgia was hunting in the back of the kitchen cupboard for the spare jar of coffee granules she knew she had somewhere when the phone in the apartment's living room rang.

'I'll get it.' Ben levered his tall, whip-thin body from the kitchen doorway, where he'd been lounging, watching her, the slow smile he gave her as sexy as his husky voice.

Returning to her search, she briefly wondered why she always blew each and every one of his suggestions of a date clean out of the water. Yet she knew why, really. It had nothing to do with him and everything to do with her.

They'd both occupied apartments on the same floor of the converted Edwardian mini-mansion in one of Birmingham's leafier suburbs for the past eight months. Returning from New York after more than six years, she'd known no one in the city, and had been grateful for the friendship Ben had offered.

He often dropped by for a chat in the evenings; sometimes, as now, to borrow something, at other times bringing a bottle of wine to share, or a recently acquired CD he thought she might like to listen to. He asked her out to dinner on an average of once a week, and apparently did not get disheartened when she consistently turned him down.

She didn't want sex rearing its ugly head and spoiling the easy friendship they had.

As she emerged from the cupboard, clutching the jar, the phone was still ringing. It had an irritable sound. She headed out of the kitchen. Ben probably couldn't find it; it would be lurking under something or other.

Which was why, as of this afternoon, she was on three weeks' leave. To finally get her apartment sorted. For eight months she'd worked her socks off, and it was time now to make a liveable home.

Ben found the phone under the pile of folded curtains she was going to hang on poles to hide the ugly chipboard doors put in by whoever had converted the building for multiple occupancy.

She heard his sexy voice turn frosty as he said to the caller, 'Yes, she is. Wait one moment.' He held out the receiver, his voice an accusation. 'It's some man. Didn't give his name.'

As if, Georgia thought wearily, no one of the male sex, apart from himself, of course, had any right to be speaking to her. Wishing again that the man/woman thing didn't make a habit of rearing up to threaten perfectly good and stable friendships, she ignored Ben's scowl and gave her name to her caller.

If it was one of her team back at the agency she didn't want to know. Her recent and highly successful presentation to the directors of a giant ice-cream manufacturing company—with not one of the men in suits finding a single fault with the storyboards or videos—had earned her the right to take part of her leave entitlement.

It wasn't one of her team. It was Jason.

Seven years, seven crowded eventful years, years of determined change and the quiet internal struggle to forget had passed since she'd seen him or heard from him. Yet his low, gravelly voice still had the power to shut her down: heartbeats, breathing, brain function, everything inside her held in frozen suspension.

So why was he calling now?

'Are you still there?'

The sudden change of tone, the stinging harshness, brought her back into the land of the living. Her breath came fast now, her heart racing, her voice all jagged edges as she confirmed, 'Of course I am. What was it you wanted?'

Hardly gracious, but there was nothing gracious or civilised about the bitterness that tainted the very blood in her veins at the sound of his voice.

He told her coldly, with no softening of his tone. 'Harold died three days ago. Suddenly, from a brain haemorrhage. The funeral's at eleven tomorrow morning. I think you should be here at Lytham, and be prepared to stay on for at least twenty-four hours.'

Georgia's skin went cold. Underneath her soft denim jeans and chunky sweater her body felt clammy. Harold? Dead? She had difficulty taking it in.

'I suppose you're having trouble deciding whether you can spare the time,' Jason said into her extended silence. 'Harold would have told me if you'd married, so I take it you have some other arrangement with the guy who answered your phone. Bring him with you if you can't do without him for a night.'

'I wouldn't inflict you and your attitude on anyone I cared about,' Georgia came back, horrified by how much his snide assumption that she couldn't bear to be without a man in her bed for one single night hurt.

'Stop being childish.' He sounded bored. 'I'm not asking you to be here for the pleasure of your company, but because you owe your stepfather respect—and rather more than that.'

'What's that supposed to mean?' What the hell was he implying?

'There's a lot to be sorted out.' He ignored her interruption. 'As I'm sure you already know, his entire estate goes to you. That means there are decisions you have to make, responsibilities you need to shoulder. I want to be sure you take them seriously—like what happens to the staff here, for instance.'

If the news of Harold's sudden death had come as a shock, the information that—for some weird reason—he had willed his entire estate to her was an even greater one. It numbed her brain for several long seconds, making her oblivious to the rest of what he was saying.

And then her mind began to buzz. Legacy or no legacy, there was no question of her staying away from his funeral. But it had been dark and raining heavily since four this afternoon, and the forecast had promised a hard frost overnight. She had no intention of risking her life—or her new sports car—on icy roads by travelling up early the following morning.

'I'll be with you in a couple of hours,' she said coldly, and ended the conversation.

If he thought she couldn't wait to get her hands on her legacy, then so be it. His opinion of her had been rock-bottom for the past seven years, so it couldn't possibly get any lower.

Whatever, it didn't matter now. How could it? She had altered beyond recognition, inside and out. She was nothing like the gullible child of seven years ago. She had worked hard to make sure that nothing could hurt her now, certainly not Jason's continuing contempt.

Yet suddenly rare tears glittered in her eyes, turning the amber to shimmering gold. Unexpected, unheralded tears for her younger self, long forgotten, for lost dreams, a lost child.

She blinked them away and straightened her spine. She never thought about the past.

'Bad news?' Ben put an arm round her shoulders.

'My stepfather died,' she answered tightly. 'I'm driving down to Gloucestershire tonight, before the roads turn into a skating rink.'

'I'm sorry.' His arm tightened around her, pulling her close. 'And who was the guy on the phone?'

'Does it matter?' she said irritably. He was acting as if he had rights in her life. Then she relented, sighing, 'Jason, my stepbrother. I hardly know him.'

And wasn't that the truth! The man that other, forgotten self had believed she loved with all her heart and soul had never really existed. Out of loneliness and lovelessness she'd created a fantasy lover, a perfect being, and had suffered for that juvenile folly. Yet for a few seconds the sound of his voice had affected her savagely, as if the dumpy teenager who had loved him for so long and so frenziedly had suddenly come alive again, and was fighting for recognition within her adult body.

Which was nonsense.

'Would you like me to drive you?' Ben asked solicitously. 'If you're in a state—it wouldn't be a problem.'

She compressed her lips, not wanting to throw his

kindness in his face, and said very politely, 'No, thank you. And, truly, I'm not in a state.'

Ben thought no woman was capable of driving, that the entire female sex should be kept off the roads by law. He'd been horrified when she'd splurged on the racy sports car she'd hankered after for years, but she was in no mood to see the funny side right now. She thrust the jar of coffee at him. 'You came for this, remember?'

'Yes, well—mind how you go. Don't drive like a maniac.'

'Stop trying to mother me.' She gritted her teeth.

'You know, or should do by now, that I don't want to be a mother to you.' His arm tightened around her shoulder again, and this time he wasn't offering comfort. 'Why don't you give me the chance to show you just what I do want to be? You never know, you might surprise yourself and like it!'

Georgia stiffened. Hadn't she told him, at least a dozen times, that she had no intention of starting a sexual relationship with him, or any other man? Ever.

Sex ruined relationships. It had made Jason treat her like a mistress for one night only and then despise her. It had made her mother resent her from practically the moment of her conception, because the man she'd been engaged to had taken to his heels when he'd learned there was a baby on the way. Vivienne had always regarded her as an unwanted encumbrance, a blight on her life.

And sex had been the only thing on Harold's mind that last fateful day at Lytham, which had ruined everything for her at the time. Yes—she had long decided she could live without sex.

She pulled briskly away from Ben. If he hadn't got the message by now he never would. She refused to waste any more breath on the subject.

'I have to pack. Close the door behind you.'

Georgia drove fast, but safely, with flair and confidence, perfectly attuned to the powerful engine beneath the long, sleek bonnet of the low-slung sports coupé.

It was like a part of herself, and when she was behind the wheel inner tension was released, the distinctive growl of the engine, as the black, aerodynamic, bullet-shaped car ate up the miles, speaking to her of freedom, taking her away from herself. Driving was the only release she allowed herself. And speed was addictive.

Headlights cut through the night, raking the wet black tarmac. She kept her foot down, stayed in the fast lane and only reluctantly eased off the accelerator slightly as she left the M5 at Brockworth and headed for deep country. And Lytham Court. And Jason.

Jason. Was he spitting tacks because he hadn't been remembered in Harold's will, full of resentment because she, the despised one, had?

And what was he expecting of her? Her mouth curled with slight, cynical amusement as she allowed herself to think about it.

A soppy sort he could push around? Someone he

could lay down the law to concerning that legacy and then walk away from, arrogantly satisfied that she would do as she was told?

And physically? If he gave that aspect a glancing thought would he expect to encounter an older version of that besotted eighteen-year-old? The billowy curves—the plague of her young life—already solidified into premature middle-age spread? Mousy hair still cropped boyishly short because she didn't know what else to do with it? Dog-like devotion swimming in her eyes, ill-fitting chainstore clothes?

Boy, was he in for a surprise!

The muted yet full-throated growl of an unfamiliar engine broke the deep silence of Lytham's isolation. Jason gathered the sheaf of papers together and pushed them back into the wall safe, locked it and pocketed the key, then walked to the open study door.

A couple of hours, she'd said. A glance at his watch confirmed she'd made it in ten minutes under. He waited. Made a conscious effort to relax coiled shoulder muscles. Waited and wondered.

Wondered if he'd manage to discuss tomorrow's funeral arrangements, and how she could best handle the huge fortune that would come into her possession after probate, without displaying the bitter contempt he felt for her.

Wondered if she would still have the nerve to look at him with big, limpid eyes. Wondered yet again how he could ever have been fooled by such a seemingly malleable sweet innocence.

Waited and wondered if she'd walk right in—this house was hers, or as good as, after all. Or would she ring the bell, as timid and self-effacing as ever, on the surface at least, yet self-seeking underneath, doing what suited her and hang the consequences?

She walked right in. She stood in the open doorway and stared at him.

He stared right back through narrowed grey eyes, unable to release the almost arrogance of her glittering golden gaze, unable to believe what he was actually seeing.

CHAPTER TWO

MEETING his eyes, Georgia sucked in her breath. Seven years had stamped authority on those harshly handsome features, on the wide-shouldered, lithe male body. And although she never looked back, not ever, there was nothing she could do now to stop her mind flying to the hollow echoes of the past. Just seeing him again made it happen...

She was eighteen years old and besottedly in love. Had loved him ever since she'd first set eyes on him at her mother's marriage to his adoptive father, Harold Harcourt, three years before.

He liked her; she knew that. On his occasional visits to Lytham Court, the luxurious family home, he made a point of spending time with her, unfailingly interested in her, always kind. And what gave her hope that liking her might develop into something more was the snippet of information that Mrs Moody, the battleaxe housekeeper, had let slip: Jason never visited Lytham while she was away at the boarding school her mother had packed her off to as soon as she'd married money.

So here she was, a naive, plump eighteen-year-old, sitting up in bed long after her mother and Harold had retired for the night, screwing up her courage to go to Jason's room and talk to him, tell him about the job offer in New York, ask him if he'd miss her—because if he said he would, she wouldn't go.

Since she'd been back at Lytham, after finishing her A levels in the early summer, Harold had been making her feel horribly uncomfortable, asking her about her boyfriends, his hot blue eyes undressing her—especially when Vivienne, her mother, wasn't around. And her mother didn't want her around; she never had. If it hadn't been for Jason's occasional visits Georgia wouldn't have spent any time here this summer, would have accepted the standing invitation to stay with her friend Sue, would have been making plans to go to New York with the family in November, making a firm decision to accept the exciting offer of a job in the new advertising agency Sue's father was setting up over there.

But how could she leave Jason? How could she go if there was even the smallest hope that he could come to love her as she loved him?

Sue's phone calls, begging her to make up her mind to go with them, were becoming more frantic. She had to reach a decision, and the only person who could help her do that was Jason.

But sitting up in bed in the thick darkness, chewing it over, wasn't going to achieve a thing! She threw back the light counterpane and slid her legs out of bed. When he'd arrived for his eagerly awaited weekend visit he'd declined the evening meal and gone to his room.

'I think I'm coming down with flu,' he'd told

them. 'The symptoms started on the way here. So I'll dose myself with aspirin and whisky and keep out of everyone's way.'

'You do that.' Vivienne had taken herself to the far side of the room, flapping her hands in front of her as if to get rid of some unspeakable contamination. 'I don't want your nasty virus! And neither does Harold!'

Harold had merely shrugged, and Georgia could have smacked the pair of them. Couldn't they see that Jason looked far from well? Didn't they care?

'I'll make a hot drink and bring it up for you, shall I?' Georgia had volunteered, determined to let him know that she, at least, cared about his state of health. 'Some soup, perhaps?'

'Thanks, poppet.' He'd smiled for the first time, his eyes brightening momentarily as they rested on her. 'But I really couldn't face it. See you in the morning.' He'd taken the whisky bottle from the drinks tray and walked out of the room, so she hadn't been able to talk to him then. But she could now.

She wouldn't disturb him for long, just explain about the job offer and tell him how she felt about him. She couldn't put the width of the Atlantic between them if there was the slightest chance he could one day return her feelings.

If he couldn't, if friendship was all he could ever offer her, then she'd make a new life for herself in America. The thought of baring her soul to him was scary, but she had to do it. Sue's parents wouldn't wait for her decision for ever.

She was shaking with nervous tension as she slipped down the corridor and into his room.

He'd fallen asleep with the bedside light on. The coward in her recognised it as a reprieve and she felt herself begin to relax, her breath coming more easily. She knew she should walk out and leave him to his healing sleep, but couldn't make herself.

She padded over to the bed, her bare feet soundless on the thick carpet, only now realising that the in-depth discussion she'd intended they have should have demanded at least the sobriety of a robe to cover the too voluptuous curves which were barely hidden by her short, thin cotton nightie.

But the night was hot and she hadn't been thinking straight, her mind rehearsing what she had to say to him over and over again. In any case, it didn't matter now. He was asleep and she wouldn't wake him.

Very carefully, her heart in her mouth, she sat on the edge of the bed. He still looked feverish, sweat gleaming on his olive-toned skin, the sheet tangled around his hips. She could smell the whisky he'd dosed himself with and realised hopelessly that she had to be grateful for the virus, for the alcohol that had knocked him out.

He was so beautiful. He could have any woman he wanted. So how could she have been crazy enough to hope for one moment that he would want her?

The sudden film of tears made her eyes sting. She blinked them away and told herself to be grateful for having been saved from a huge humiliation.

If he'd been awake and she'd come out with all that stuff she would have embarrassed them both; she could see that very clearly now. His past friendship and kindnesses meant only one thing—that he was compassionate enough to care about the plain, over-plump teenager who was like a fish out of water in the opulence of Lytham Court, whose mother plainly showed she didn't want her around.

So she would go to New York and make something of her life, but first she would give herself this quiet, secret time with the man she loved with an emotion so intense it made her heart feel heavy and sharp inside her. Just a few more minutes to say her silent goodbyes.

Tears shimmering on her lashes, she softly, oh, so softly, touched his naked shoulder. The last thing she wanted to do was wake him, but she needed to have the memory of how his skin felt beneath her loving fingers.

He was burning, feverish. She lifted her hand and laid the backs of her fingers against his brow, where strands of damp, dark hair tumbled onto his forehead, then feathered them gently over his jagged cheekbones, down to the corner of his mouth, and then, because she simply couldn't stop herself, trailed her hand over the taut muscles of his arm, down to the loosely clenched long bones of his hand, completely absorbed in him.

And then, in the space of time it took to draw a breath, his eyes opened, his fingers tightened convulsively around hers, drawing her hand up until her palm was splayed against his wide chest and she could feel the rapid, heavy beats of his heart.

After that there was no time to explain what she was doing in his room as his mouth descended in a bone-melting kiss. No time to think as she drowned giddily in a vortex of passion, his passion and hers, the driven need taking them both by storm.

She didn't have to ask if he could ever love her. He had given her the answer.

She woke in her own bed, but couldn't remember climbing back into it. Had Jason carried her here? She was filled with the scatty kind of happiness that made her heart soar up to the skies and dance around the sun. Jason's lovemaking had been more beautiful than anything she could ever have imagined. He couldn't have been so passionate if he didn't love her.

She floated down to breakfast, her head spinning. Today they would talk. There were decisions to be made about New York, although what had happened last night made them academic. Her future was here with the man she loved.

The elegantly furnished dining room was empty. A glance at her watch told her she was too early. Mrs Moody didn't serve breakfast before nine-thirty. Her mother and stepfather weren't early risers.

She smiled softly, her amber eyes jewel-bright. She would take Jason's breakfast up on a tray. Juice, toast, honey and coffee. They could talk in privacy. And when she told him she loved him he would tell her he felt the same, and kiss her, and maybe invite her to share his bed, and undress her slowly, and then...

Her heart was beating so fast she thought she might suffocate, and the heat of desire scorched her skin. She turned quickly, heading for the door and the kitchen. And Jason walked in.

She couldn't speak, could only look at him with drowning, love-drenched eyes, one hand flying to her breast to still the wild clamouring of her heart. He looked pale, as if the night had taken the colour from his skin, making his slate-grey eyes darker by contrast, emphasising the lines of strain at the side of his beautiful male mouth.

He raked his fingers through his soft dark hair, a track Georgia longed to follow with her own fingers. But she knew she shouldn't be thinking of things like that when he obviously wasn't well.

'Let me get you something,' she said, concern in her eyes. 'Coffee, juice, eggs—anything.'

But he shook his head, briefly closing his eyes so that the thick dark sweep of his lashes laid sooty crescents above his jutting, harshly masculine cheekbones.

Then he looked at her, and she saw regret in his eyes, heard it in his voice when he told her, 'About last night. I'm more sorry than I can say for what happened. I'm fond of you; you know that, Georgia. The last thing I want to do is hurt you.'

'You didn't!' she gasped. 'How could you think that? Last night—' Her face flamed at the wholly erotic memory, at the vision of the new and totally unexpected world he'd opened up for her. She swallowed convulsively. 'Last night was the most beautiful thing that has ever happened to me.'

She ached to go to him, to lean her head against the broad expanse of his chest, but there was something forbidding about his hard features that kept her feet rooted to the carpet. She felt emotional tears sting her eyes again as she protested, 'Please don't be sorry about what happened. I can't bear it. It was all my fault; you know it was.' And it *was* her fault; of course it was. She shouldn't have let it happen. She'd taken advantage of him while he was at his most vulnerable.

'No.' He turned away from her, his hands bunched into the pockets of his narrow-fitting jeans, his shoulders rigid beneath the stone-coloured sweatshirt he was wearing. 'The blame is mine entirely. I'm eight years older. I should have had more control, dammit! Packed you back to your own room and your teddy bears!'

'Don't say that—I'm not a child!' The words were torn from her heart. She was losing everything she'd dared to believe she'd gained. Losing him. It couldn't happen. She wouldn't let it happen! 'Jason—I love you! Don't you understand?'

He swung round to face her then, slowly, on the balls of his feet, his features less harsh, some softer emotion hazing his eyes so that for a tiny moment her heart lifted with hope, only to be shot down again when he countered gently, 'Believe me, you only think you do. Last night—it was your first time.'

Dull colour flared briefly over his broad, ruggedly defined cheekbones, but his eyes didn't waver, holding hers intently as if by his will alone he could force her to accept what he wanted her to believe.

'That being so, it's only natural that you should imagine—'

'I don't "imagine"! Give me some credit!' The sheer vehemence of her interruption wiped the unhappy mixture of shame and compassion from his face. And his eyes narrowed watchfully as she went on, 'I fell in love with you the first time I ever saw you, and I've loved you ever since!' He had to know how real it was, how true and strong her love for him. He mustn't think she'd made love with him on a whim.

Her chin jutting out, she defied him to say she was lying. He didn't, just sounded drained and weary as he told her gently, 'You're eighteen years old, Georgia. And for this day and age incredibly innocent. If you feel anything for me at all it can't be anything other than infatuation.' He reached out a hand as if to touch her, then withdrew it, thrust it back in his pocket. 'Believe me, my dear, you're still too young to really understand your own feelings. And I'm not prepared to take any more advantage of your innocence than I already have. Try to forget it ever happened. You have the whole of your life ahead of you, and if it's worth anything at all to you, I'll be around for you if you ever need me. You know that.'

He left the room without another word, without a backward glance, and left Lytham an hour later.

The pain of his going was unspeakable.

She spent the next few weeks in a pit of misery, moping around the house, irritating her mother, making Harold give her knowing little winks and leers.

'Don't nag her, Vivvie. She's pining for some boy; it's obvious! Did he dump you, sweetheart? He's a fool if he did—a curvy little handful like you!'

And still she couldn't bring herself to get away. She'd told Sue and her parents that she'd decided to take up their offer, but hadn't bothered to obey her friend's telephoned command to, 'Get your butt over to our place and we can make plans about what we're going to do when we hit the Big Apple—provided Dad gives us any time off from our dogsbody jobs at the agency!'

For the first time ever, giggly girl-talk with the bubbly Sue held no appeal whatsoever.

She was waiting for Jason. Hoping he'd rethink his rejection, telling herself that he wasn't trying to avoid her, that he might have had another disagreement with Harold. They'd never seemed close—just as she and her mother weren't. Or maybe he was just too busy to come. Recently accepted as a junior partner in a prestigious firm of London solicitors which specialised in fraud in high places, he could be too focused on his work to find time to visit.

But in her heart she knew the excuses she made were futile. He didn't come because he just didn't want to have to see her again.

On the point of capitulating to Sue's demands, telling her mother of her future plans and packing her bags, she made a discovery that shook her out of her torpor.

She was pregnant!

She panicked. She didn't know what to do. Vivienne would show her no sympathy or understanding whatsoever, and would almost certainly urge her to have an abortion. And as for Harold, she couldn't bear to encounter his knowing, hot eyes.

Jason was the only one she could turn to, because hadn't he said he'd be there for her if she needed him? And hadn't he helped to create this new life she was carrying inside her?

She phoned his London number late at night, when she was sure he'd be at his apartment. It took every ounce of courage she possessed. After she'd told him she held her breath, feeling her pulse-rate rise.

But all he said was, 'I take it you're sure?'

'I wouldn't be phoning—'

'OK. Calm down. I'll be with you first thing in the morning. We'll make plans. And Georgia—don't worry.'

As if she could help it!

She lay awake all night, wondering if his plans would include a discreet abortion, and knew that she would never, ever be pressured into ending the life of her unborn child. He or she would be a part of Jason she would have for ever. And she'd think about the practicalities of raising a child on her own when the dust had settled.

Jason arrived at Lytham at eight the next morning, well before Harold and Vivienne were up, declining Mrs Moody's stiffly formal offer of breakfast. The housekeeper never spoke unless it was necessary, and Georgia had never seen her smile, but the look she shot between the two of them now spoke volumes.

So Jason took her arm and walked her out of the impressive house and into the garden, which was manicured to within an inch of its life.

'We'll marry just as soon as it can be arranged.' Marriage to Jason was all she had ever yearned for. Her heart skittered around like a wild thing, then settled down to a heavy, solemn beat. She sat down abruptly on an over-ornate cast-iron bench seat, sweat breaking out on her short upper lip as she forced out, 'You don't have to.'

'I know I don't have to. No one's holding a gun to my head.'

He was standing over her, his back to the morning sun, his face in shadow so she couldn't read his expression. Yet she knew it would be as bleak and emotionless as his voice.

'It's the only option,' he told her tonelessly. 'A termination's out of the question, so don't even think about it. I'm the father, and I'm responsible for both you and the baby. My child will have the best possible start in life, and a stable background with both parents as permanent fixtures. And that means marriage.'

It was what she wanted, but would it work? He

didn't love her, and if she hadn't been pregnant he would have avoided her where possible.

She twisted her fingers together in her lap and he told her, 'I can't stay, I've got a hell of a lot on at the moment, but during this coming week I'll arrange the date and venue for the ceremony. After the wedding you can move in with me, and when I'm less pushed for time we'll look for somewhere more suitable. A city apartment's not the ideal environment for a child.'

As proposals went, this one rated rather less than one out of ten. She clamped her lips together to stop them quivering, and he said, his voice gentling, 'It will be all right; I promise. We'll make a good marriage.' Briefly, he reached out to ruffle her boyishly cropped hair. 'I have to go now, but I'll be back a week today, early evening. We'll break the news to the parents over dinner. Don't say anything until then. If there's any flak flying, I'll take it.'

A good marriage. If he was willing to make it work then so was she. But to be the wife of a successful young solicitor she needed to change her image, and she spent most of the week hunting for suitable clothes, because how could he be proud of a wife who went around wearing fault-concealing baggy trousers and tops?

It was the afternoon, a week later, before she found the perfect dress for dinner that evening. She wanted to wear something that would make a statement, to appear older and more sophisticated in front of

Harold and Vivienne, and to show Jason she was more than prepared to make an effort.

Hurrying into the house through the kitchen regions, clutching the classy carriers, she encountered Mrs Moody.

'Mrs Harcourt's been looking for you. You'll find her in the conservatory.'

'Thanks.' No need to say more. Mrs Moody didn't encourage chit-chat. For the first time ever Georgia didn't feel intimidated by the severe mouth, the glacial, disapproving eyes. And as she sped up to her suite of rooms to get ready for Jason, for the announcement he would make over dinner tonight, her confidence soared. Vivienne could wait; she had more important things to do than listen to her endless complaints.

When her mother had married Harold Harcourt, after meeting him when she'd worked as his temporary personal secretary, Georgia had been overawed, intimidated, even, by the opulence of this house and Harold's staggering wealth. Unused to anything of the kind, she'd been out of her depth, afraid of putting a foot wrong.

But her mother had taken to her new lifestyle as if she'd been born to it, instead of having had to scratch a living to support herself and her unwanted child. She lapped up the luxury of having everything done for her, more designer clothes than she could wear, and a holiday home in the Caribbean.

Well, Vivienne was welcome to it! Georgia was about to embark on a life of her own, with Jason and their baby. Very carefully, she took the black dress from one of the carriers and laid it across her bed.

Classy. Jersey silk and cut on the bias, so it clung in the right places. Short—four inches above her knees—with a scoopy bodice. When she'd tried it on it had made her look sleek, yet voluptuous, rather than just plain overweight.

And plain black courts in the softest leather imaginable, with high and slender heels to give extra height to her perpendicularly challenged frame. She'd stopped growing when she reached five-two—upwardly, anyway.

After her shower she anointed her body with perfume, musky, exotic and disgracefully expensive. To give him his due, Harold made her a generous allowance. She rarely touched it, but today she'd dipped deep into her account.

But it had been worth it, she thought as she wriggled into the scraps of scarlet nonsense that passed as underwear. Used to wearing sturdy, practical undies, she found her mirror image a blush-making revelation.

The low-cut bra lovingly shaped her breasts, displaying them to their full advantage, and the tiny briefs emphasised her sex. Would Jason want her if he saw her like this? Would he see her as a desirable woman instead of a graceless lump? Would he decide that marriage to her might be more exciting than a mere execution of his duty? Would he think she was sexy?

The unmistakable sound of someone entering the

adjoining bedroom sent her already thudding heartbeats into a frenzy. No one ever came to her rooms, not even Mrs Moody, because she looked after them herself.

Jason?

Her hand fluttered to her throat. It had to be him. He'd promised to be here in time for dinner. With an hour still to go he could have decided to speak to her privately before announcing their marriage plans later on.

Her eyes widening, her veins racing with fire, she watched the porcelain knob of the bathroom door make a slow half-turn.

A few short weeks ago she would have been diving for a towel to cover her near-nakedness, and she almost gave in to the impulse now, but managed not to because there was no earthly reason to be shy with the man she loved with every atom of her being, the man who would soon be her husband, the man who had fathered the new and precious life she was carrying.

And she would have the answers to the questions she'd asked herself only a few seconds ago!

Then the world went black and very still. Harold stood in the open doorway, staring at her. And Georgia stared back, too shocked and embarrassed to move.

The way he was looking at her made her feel like throwing up. His heavy face was red, hot eyes raking over every inch of her body. She tried to make a move, to grab a towel from the rail and cover herself, but her feet seemed to have grown roots through the floor.

'Well, well, well—what an eye-opener!'

He was leering at her, Georgia thought, horrified. Oh, if only she weren't so gauche, knew how to handle this hateful situation. 'You have been hiding your light under a bushel!'

The thick sound of his voice galvanised her, was all it took to have her leaping over the tiles, grabbing for a towel. But Harold side-stepped, moving quickly for a heavy man, and was there before her, mocking, 'No need to be shy with me, sweetie. No need at all.'

Beginning to panic now, she couldn't agree with that. He might only be teasing, indulging in one of his too-near-the-bone jokes at her expense, but she wouldn't bet on it. And the only way to stop his eyes crawling all over her body was to cover it.

She made a desperate lunge for the edge of the bathtowel she could see behind his bulky frame and he caught her before she made the connection, his laugh high and silly, his hands grabbing, all over her.

And then all hell broke loose.

At any other time the sight of her mother's distorted features would have struck her as being hysterically funny, the twisted expression on her expertly made-up face and the raucous tone of her voice an almost surreal contrast to the perfect taste of the smoke-grey silk that hung so beautifully on her pin-thin body.

'Just what the hell is going on in here? Hal? Answer me, Hal!'

Her flesh crawling with embarrassment, Georgia found herself thrust aside. She was shaking all over, not knowing what to do or say, grateful that the hateful mauling had stopped but horrified that her mother should have witnessed the degrading scene.

This was the worst thing that had ever happened to her, she thought wildly, and then proved herself wrong, because Jason was here, too, his face dark with bitter anger, and that had to be worse than anything she could possibly have imagined. 'Vivvie, sweetheart,' Harold said. 'Don't get the wrong end of the stick!'

He smoothed a hand over his thinning hair and Georgia just knew he would have straightened his tie had he been wearing one.

'I hate to have to tell you this, but I can't have you getting all the wrong ideas—I only came up here to pass on that message her friend left with you. That Sue somebody-or-other who's been phoning all afternoon. Thought I'd save you the trouble, darling. But this little minx of yours was parading about in those skimpy things.' He drew his brows down in an anxious frown. 'I haven't said anything before—didn't want to upset you—but she's been coming on to me for weeks now. And just now—well—she just threw herself at me, as you must have seen for yourself.'

All eyes on her, condemning her, Georgia could barely hold herself upright, let alone speak.

How could Harold say such disgusting things

about her? She was shaking so badly, inside and out, that her denial when it came was barely audible.

'I didn't. No, I didn't!'

She knew she hadn't sounded convincing, and her mother was shouting at her, the words she said scrambled by her own panicking brain, making no sense. But she could tell by the look of loathing in Vivienne's eyes that she didn't believe her.

And why should she? Why should she believe the truth when it would mean that her marriage would never be the same again? Why sacrifice wealth, luxury and ease if by blinkering herself she didn't have to?

And the look of deep and bitter contempt on Jason's face said it all. He didn't believe her, either. The offer of marriage had been made out of duty. He didn't love her, never had and never could, and now he despised her. He had only let her into his bed because she'd been eager and offering herself.

Hadn't Sue's mother once asked, 'Why are men ruled by their hormones?' shaking her head over her twenty-year-old son's latest folly. Guy had been chasing after a woman from the nearby village, twice his age, and rumoured to be no better than she should be.

Jason had been ruled by his hormones, his judgement clouded by alcohol, and now deeply—and probably bitterly—regretted it. If he thought anything of her at all he would be defending her now, at least asking to hear her side of the story.

But he didn't say a word, and she just knew that

this farce gave him the perfect get-out. If he believed Harold, he could free himself up to believe anything—believe that after her initiation she had thrown herself at every male she came across, greedy for sex, allow himself to believe that the child she was carrying wasn't even his!

Blinded by a sudden deluge of tears, she stumbled from the room, her arms crossed tightly across her breasts in a vain and belated attempt to hide as much of herself and her stupid red underwear as she could from Jason's bleak, contemptuous eyes.

He made no move to stop her, or to follow her, and the last tiny flicker of hope snuffed out and died. And as she scrabbled around in her bedroom, snatching up the jeans and sweater she'd discarded earlier, her shoes and handbag, she could hear the low, harsh sound of his voice, her mother's shrill tirade, Harold's low, placating mutters.

They would be discussing her gross behaviour, she decided hysterically, heading for the door. Deciding how to get her contaminating presence out of their lives.

She fled down the corridor until she could no longer hear their voices, pulled her clothes on, walked into her shoes and clattered down the stairs.

As she reversed the small car she had been given the use of out of the garage, with more speed than precision, she knew exactly where she would go. To Sue.

Mercifully, she'd been too busy wandering round the shops planning her future with Jason to even think about contacting her friend to tell her what had happened and that she'd changed her mind about going with them to New York after all.

Kate and Robin Ansley, Sue's parents, wouldn't turn their backs on her, she knew that. Though at the moment they were both in New York. Robin had been there for weeks, setting up the American branch of his London-based advertising agency, and now Kate had flown out for a couple of weeks to make the final decision about where the family should live.

They had always welcomed her into their close and loving family, and would do everything they could to support her through this; she knew that. And Sue would fight her corner to the bitter end.

CHAPTER THREE

GEORGIA came back to the present with a jolt. She felt numb all over, the rapid playback of the past stunning her brain. And the way Jason was looking at her now, with contempt and scarcely veiled hostility, told her that Harold had never owned up to the truth of what had happened that evening all those years ago.

Maybe he'd meant to, but had never raked up enough courage. Jason could be frighteningly forbidding when he wanted to be.

But she'd made her peace with her mother's husband a long time ago. He'd flown out to New York to break the news of her mother's death in a car accident the day after her funeral. She hadn't wanted to see him, not after what he'd done, but his altered appearance had shocked her so much she had listened to what he'd had to say.

His wife's death, and the manner of it, had made him take a long, hard look at himself, and he'd hated what he'd seen. He hadn't been able to apologise enough for the lies he'd told on that traumatic evening, the damage he'd done to her, and ultimately to his wife.

It had been hard to forgive him, but, faced with someone as obviously tormented by guilt as he was, she'd had no option but to try. On his return to England he'd written often, and occasionally she had replied, and when she'd returned to the UK he'd travelled to Birmingham once a month to give her lunch.

She'd cancelled their last date, though. She'd been so busy with her presentation. Now she wished she'd made time. He'd always seemed so lonely, pathetically pleased to have her company. He'd never known about her pregnancy, and that had made things easier because not knowing, he couldn't mention it.

Jason was tall, over six feet, and she had to tilt her chin up to look him in the face. There was nothing there to see but naked dislike. Did he ever wonder what had happened to their baby? Did he even care? Had Vivienne told him about the miscarriage, or had neither of them bothered to mention the subject?

He'd made no attempt to contact her in all these years. He'd washed his hands of her, and the child she'd been carrying.

She never allowed herself to think about the miscarriage, the lost baby; it hurt too much. She closed her eyes briefly, to hide the pain, and felt his gaze on her like a brand, burning through her eyelids. She snapped them open again, and stared into the hard, hostile eyes, pushing the past firmly away. She didn't know this man who had ignored her existence, the fate of their child. And didn't want to.

The change in her stunned him. He was staring, he knew he was, but could do nothing about it.

This new version of the plump teenager he remembered was stylishly slender, yet perfectly formed, wearing an elegantly simple cream-coloured sweater, which almost certainly carried an Italian label, over narrow-fitting designer jeans. The woman she had become was light years away from the dumpy, frumpy fifteen-year-old he had first met at Harold and Vivienne's wedding ten years ago.

The first real and deep compassion he'd felt in all of his twenty-three years of living had twisted sharply inside his guts as he'd looked at her then, wearing an awful blue satin dress that had emphasised every bulge, a fluffy confection of blue flowers set incongruously and precariously on her mouse-brown cropped head, and carrying her mother's bouquet of white lilies in hands that visibly shook.

There'd been a look of bewilderment in her huge eyes that had made him want to take care of her, shelter her from life's knocks. Especially when Vivienne, elegant in a darker blue silk, had raised a perfectly arched, perfectly derisive eyebrow whenever her hapless daughter made a gauche remark or clumsy movement.

Vivienne had had no time for her daughter, he had sensed that from the start, and later he had learned why.

But Georgia's uncomfortably awkward smile—when he had eventually persuaded her to give one—had been beautiful, trusting and innocent, her eyes clinging to his as if he'd been a rock in a raging sea.

Now there was no compassion in him, not for her.

She had killed any care he had had for her as surely as she had killed their child. He'd felt sick to his soul when Vivienne had told him of the abortion.

Besides, from the look of her, she needed none. And her smile—should she ever decide to thaw that haughty expression—might still be as beautiful as sunrise, but it would leave him cold.

She broke the long silence. 'I need the remote control thingy to open the garages.' Car keys dangled from one slim finger. She'd done something to her hair. Long now, cascading to her shoulders, it shimmered and gleamed in the overhead lights. It looked as soft as the costliest of silks.

Hooding his eyes, he strode towards her, held out a hand. 'I'll garage it for you and bring in your luggage.'

'No.' Instinctively she enclosed the keys in the palm of her hand. 'No one touches that car but me.'

So there was an area where she was vulnerable. He shrugged. What did he care? He followed her out, and the vehicle in front of the closed garage area did raise an eyebrow. No wonder she was possessive.

Powerful, sexy, beautifully styled, its origins were as obvious as the classy sweater she wore. Either her job paid mega-bucks or she had a rich lover.

From the look of her, and what he knew of her, from what he remembered of the way she was in bed, he'd lay odds on the sugar daddy. He activated the remote control, then tossed it to her and instructed tightly, 'Lock up after you. You're in your old room. Supper in ten minutes; Mrs Moody held it back.'

He'd been watching the double doors slide open as he spoke, and now he turned to look at her again. Her hair shimmered under the security lights and her eyes were dark amber pools that said, Arrogant bastard! as clearly as if she'd spoken the words aloud.

He acknowledged the challenge, the confrontational gauntlet thrown down by those unwavering golden eyes with a brief dip of his head, a tight smile, then strode back into the house.

She could find her own way. Whatever else she might have forgotten—her morals, her responsibilities towards the new life she had once carried and, yes, to him—she could hardly have forgotten the way to the suite of rooms that had been hers. And she could carry her own bags.

Politeness cost nothing, but now he wasn't even prepared to give her that. Had she been as unsure of herself, as outwardly quashed as he remembered, then he might have been able to manage a stilted pretence of polite behaviour. But this new sassy, super-confident creature with the gleam of battle in her eyes could expect nothing from him.

After the funeral, after he'd satisfied himself that she was prepared to take her new responsibilities seriously, Georgia Blake was on her own.

Her old room. Georgia flung it a look of deep distaste.

She had always hated the little-girly pinks and peaches Vivienne had chosen for its decor, the frills and flounces everywhere and the delicate white and gold furniture that looked as if it might fall to pieces if she went anywhere near it. She had felt like a lumbering elephant in a fairy grotto, but had been too unsure of herself, too cowed by her mother's resentment of her existence, to object.

If Jason had possessed any sensitivity at all he would have asked Mrs Moody to make a bed up for her in one of the several guest rooms.

Thankfully, she would only have to make use of the room that had been the scene of her humiliation and anguish for a couple of nights at most. Thankfully again, a quick inspection revealed that all of the things she'd left behind on that terrible evening had been turfed out of the drawers and hanging cupboards. Mrs Moody would have binned them on her mother's instructions.

She tossed her overnight bag on the frilly pink bedcover and stood in front of the mirror, running her fingers through her untidy mane of hair.

'Mouse' was a thing of the past. After the trauma of losing everything—Jason, their baby, the right to show her face at Lytham, to have anything more to do with her mother—her hair had grown because she simply hadn't bothered to have it cut, and the puppy fat had dropped off her because she had only been able to pick at her food.

A final fleeting glance told her she'd do. Jason would have to take her as she was. Vivienne had always insisted they dress for dinner. How well she remembered having to climb out of her uniform of baggy tops that hid a multitude of sins and deck herself in the frilly frocks her mother deemed suitable for a young girl.

Or perhaps Vivienne had deliberately picked out those awful fussy dresses because she'd known they made her daughter look a fright, the contrast with her own elegant perfection all the more pointed.

She wouldn't let it hurt her. Why should she? Vivienne was dead, the past was dead, and Jason—despite appearing as handsome and virile as ever; even more so if she were to be painfully honest—might just as well be.

Being at Lytham again brought back far too many uncomfortable memories, and if what Jason had said about her inheritance was true then she'd get rid of the place faster than it took her gorgeous, powerful new car to get from nought to sixty!

She found him in the breakfast room, and he hadn't changed what he was wearing, either. So the old order had altered. Which, she thought, raking her eyes over the lean, powerful frame enhanced by his casual jeans and sweater, was a pity. She would have taken perverse pleasure from annoying him, underlining her confident independence.

'Ready to eat?' Did she have to look at him as if they were squaring up for the fight of the century? He lifted the lid of the steaming casserole Mrs Moody had brought through five minutes ago, along with a clutch of jacket potatoes, and found the enticing aroma repelled him.

'I'm not hungry,' Georgia stated, helping herself from the opened bottle of red wine, filling a glass for him, making it look like a slightly insulting afterthought, before carrying her own drink to one of the armchairs that flanked the brightly burning fire. 'But you go ahead.'

Bitch! he thought savagely, but held his tongue. Who would have thought the vulnerable, too-eager-to-please Georgia would have grown up into—into this? But then who would have thought that that same, seemingly loving child-woman would have coldly and callously aborted their baby without even consulting him?

He put the cover back on the untouched casserole and pulled out one of the dining chairs, angling it to face her. Time to get any necessary talking out of the way: details of tomorrow's funeral, the exact extent of her very considerable inheritance, and a lecture on her responsibilities to the resident staff if she decided to liquidise her property assets.

Instead he found himself deriding, 'Is that how you stay thin? By starving yourself? There was a time when you'd eat everything you could lay your hands on.'

The forbidding, steely eyes, the dark, slashing frown would have sent the old Georgia running to hide. The new one was unquenchable, and it was high time he got to understand that.

'Not thin, surely?' With deliberate provocation she ran one hand slowly over her body, drawing attention to the pert swell of her breasts, the very feminine curve of her hip. 'Let's say slender.' Her gaze was coolly mocking and Jason's breath hissed in his throat as he silently amended 'bitch' to 'witch'.

She had matured into one very sexy lady. But outward appearances meant nothing. He preferred the admittedly over-generous curves of the extraordinarily loving body that had been his for that brief time, when a combination of medicinal drugs and a hefty dose of alcohol had made him forget that he was supposed to be a responsible adult.

Memories of that amazing night, so rigorously denied for seven years, punched holes in his brain, and he drained his wine glass, wishing it were something stronger, as she told him languorously, 'Normally I have a healthy appetite, I assure you. The difference is, I no longer go in for comfort eating.'

That made sense; he had to admit that. The kid had had a loveless, largely lonely life, packed off to boarding school and encouraged, when possible, to spend as much time during the holidays with her schoolfriend—all because the elegant Vivienne hadn't wanted her teenage daughter to clutter up her new, sophisticated lifestyle.

He remembered arriving for the weekend, one summer Saturday morning, and finding Georgia in the kitchen, her face red with guilt and covered with crumbs, being lectured by Mrs Moody for polishing off a whole batch of newly baked cookies.

He didn't want to remember feeling sorry for her. Or the way he'd cast around for something to take her mind off the humiliating scene he'd walked in on, telling her he was stiff from driving, suggesting she accompany him on a walk over the fields. He didn't want to remember anything about her.

It was his own fault, of course, for mentioning something as personal as her eating habits. He regretted the lack of control that had led to the remark. It wouldn't happen again.

'Right.' Briefly, unemotionally, he detailed the arrangements for tomorrow's funeral, then commented, his tone unaltered, 'As you didn't bother to attend your mother's funeral I can only assume you're here for your stepfather's because he discussed the contents of his will with you. However—'

'Hold it!' The cool detachment dropped away as she pushed herself to her feet and slapped her almost empty wine glass down on the table. She stared down at him, her wide mouth tight. 'I was out of the city on business and knew nothing of Vivienne's death until Harold flew out to New York the day after her funeral, so you can button your lip on the snide remarks. And, no, you choose to assume wrongly; Harold never discussed his will or his financial affairs with me.'

'No?' One black brow arched, grey eyes cool, cynical. 'Then what did you discuss during your cosy little lunches? Or would you rather not tell me? Did you know,' he said flatly, almost uninterestedly, 'that he kept all the letters you wrote him from New York?'

What the hell did he think he was implying? Emotion, raw and sharp, tore ragged holes around her heart. She was right; Harold had obviously never put the record straight. Jason thought now, as he had done then, that she'd enthusiastically thrown herself at anything in trousers.

Over the years she'd worked so hard to block out any sign of emotion where he was concerned. She had confidently believed she'd managed it, that the only emotion she could feel for him was a cool and distant contempt. Showing any emotion in front of him, even anger, was a definite no-no.

As he tipped the bottle to refill her glass she pulled in a deep breath and made a conscious effort to unclamp her jaws. He couldn't get to her; she wouldn't let him.

Controlled again now, she responded evenly, 'You found my letters, so I'm sure you read them through a microscope.'

She hoped he had; she did so hope he had. Duty things, and not many of them, written because she'd felt sorry for the lonely, guilt-ridden elderly man, and because it had seemed unmannerly not to reply to one or two of the dozens he'd sent her. Duty letters. Nothing in them but comments about her work, the weather.

But he didn't tell her whether he'd read them or not, and she reminded herself that she didn't care a fig what he thought of her and watched him push her glass towards her over the smooth, polished surface of the table.

'Forget it.' He sounded bored with the subject. 'Take your wine and sit down. If you really don't know, then I'll run over the details of his will for you.'

She shrugged, just slightly, took the glass, but didn't sit down. The time when she would have walked over hot coals if he'd told her to was long since past. She wandered over to the window instead, tweaked aside the heavy claret-coloured curtains and gazed up at a billion stars. It was freezing hard, but the atmosphere inside was much, much colder as Jason stated matter-of-factly, 'Everything he had comes to you. As you know, on his marriage to your mother he sold his company—I'd already told him I had no interest in property development. The proceeds were wisely invested, so he leaves an extremely healthy portfolio. The interest on the investments means you would never have to work again if you didn't want to. And this house, of course, and everything in it. I can't see you keeping it on, and imagine you would prefer to sell.'

He watched her closely. Her profile, cameoed against the black of the night sky, could have been carved from marble. No reaction. No pretence of being overwhelmed by such largesse. Not even a flicker of avarice. Unlike her younger self—transparent as tap water—this new Georgia played her cards very close to her chest.

He pushed aside an unwilling respect, and wondered if his next pronouncement might produce a reaction. 'Since Harold failed to do so, I suggest you think about making provision for Mrs Moody if you do decide to sell after probate. She's looked after things here very efficiently for as long as I can remember. I know she's not exactly a bundle of fun, but she means well. At her age she's not likely to find another job with living accommodation. Think about it. Then, of course, there's Baines. He's done the gardens for the past thirty-odd years on ridiculously low wages. He and his wife have their own small cottage, so he won't have so much to lose as Mrs Moody. But I would suggest he deserves something.'

That got a reaction, proving—if he'd needed proof—that his assessment of her character was spot-on. He knew it when she slowly turned her head, looking at him with cold golden eyes, her delicate nostrils slightly flared, her wide mouth curved with a slight, contemptuous smile.

'Anyone else in need of a hand-out? You, perhaps? I would imagine so, since Harold didn't make provision for you, either. How much would you like? Would half be enough? Or do you think you should have it all?'

She didn't regret a word. Not a single one. He was Harold's adopted son; naturally he would bitterly resent everything going to her, the pariah. But she wasn't about to show misgivings in front of this man who had so decisively turned his back on her at the time when she'd needed him most.

And of course she would ensure Mrs Moody and Baines received generous recognition for their years of loyalty and service, but she had no intention of telling him that, and letting him think he still had the power to pull her strings. She'd hoped her scathing comments had made him feel small, and was so appalled when she saw him lean back on his chair and actually smile that she had to look away.

'You're welcome to the lot,' he told her smoothly. 'I make my own way. I even funded my years at university with a legacy my mother left in trust. I took nothing of Harold's after I reached eighteen, and I want nothing of his now. As I said, you're welcome to it.' The derisive smile slid away, his mouth going tight. 'I'm sure you more than earned it.'

'If you say so.' She lifted one shoulder in a tiny shrug to indicate complete indifference, to show him he could no longer wound her with his rock-bottom opinions.

She drained the wine in her glass. She needed something to help her sleep. Then wished she hadn't because it made her feel peculiar.

'If that's it, I think I'll turn in.'

She began to head towards the door, slowly, her legs feeling a bit like cotton wool now, and Jason, watching her impassively, said, 'Not quite.'

Her progress halted, Georgia grasped the back of a chair to steady herself. The floor seemed to be dipping and swaying under her feet. 'What now?' she asked belligerently. She couldn't let him see she was tipsy, would loathe the consequent scornful amusement.

'Blue Rock,' he said. He watched her unwillingly. She was pale, her huge eyes wide, burning. Suddenly she looked practically out on her feet. She was too sophisticated a being to be affected by a couple of glasses of wine. Over-excited by her prospects, he guessed. Meeting up with him again wouldn't have had that effect because she didn't have a conscience. Well, he'd give her something else to get excited about.

'The island, the house, and everything in it. Harold never went back after the accident. Apparently, Vivienne left a lot of personal stuff behind. I doubt you'd be interested in her clothes, but you might like to get your hands on her jewellery.' He got to his feet. He'd had enough of her company, as much as he could take. 'If you feel like flying out, taking the boyfriend, you'd be well looked after. Blossom and Elijah still live in the annexe and look after the house.'

The room was so quiet he could hear her breathing. Sharing space with her made his blood run hot. Suddenly, the thought of her taking up his suggestion, spending time on the island with her current boyfriend—the guy who'd answered her phone?—made every muscle in his body go into spasm.

The pigeons were coming home to roost with a vengeance, and he had no one to blame but himself. He'd behaved with reckless irresponsibility, lived through the traumatic consequences, managed to put the whole thing behind him.

Or so he'd thought.

Seeing her in the flesh, gorgeous, sexy, self-possessed, awoke something raw and savage inside himself. He wanted to lash out at her for being so damned fanciable, at himself for finding her so, at fate for pushing them together again.

He said a brusque goodnight and walked out of the room. He didn't look at her. He couldn't. Looking at her created a pain it was impossible to describe.

CHAPTER FOUR

THE dream had been haunting her far less regularly. But that night she dreamed of the baby. The baby that was dead.

She woke and felt the weight of guilt, and wept, and couldn't stop. The dream had been more heart-wrenching because of its long absence.

At the funeral, at the gathering of the handful of mourners back at the house, she kept the tears inside her, silent, smothered, but no less real. She couldn't weep for Harold, with whom she had made her peace; the silent tears were for her baby, with whom she had not, and never would while the guilt stayed with her. If only she hadn't allowed herself to get so distraught over what had happened, over Harold's lies and Jason's contempt, she might not have miscarried, she might have kept her baby!

She'd done her best to hide the ravages of her restless, grieving night, used far more make-up than usual, worn a slate-grey business suit with a white silk scarf tucked into the neckline. But her face felt unnaturally stiff, like stone, and she caught the penetrating appraisal of Jason's grey and narrowed eyes and wondered if he knew the reason for her grief.

But of course he didn't. He'd turned that strong, broad back on her and their baby, shut them out of his mind. He didn't know what had happened to the child he had fathered—apart from Sue, and her loving, supportive family, no one did.

And he hadn't even asked, didn't want to know. Didn't want to know if he'd fathered a boy or a girl, if the child was doing well at school, happy and strong. If the child was alive.

The pain of it nagged her like an aching tooth, an abscess eating away at an exposed nerve. The pain wouldn't go away and so she knew *she* must, and as quickly as possible.

She saw Jason escort the last of the mourners out through the hall and began to stack plates and glasses on to a tray. She carried it through to the kitchen.

Mrs Moody, her small eyes red-rimmed, folded her hands across her stomach and said, 'You don't need to do that; it's my job—while I still have a job.'

'That's what I'd like to talk about.'

Georgia put the heavy tray down on one of the gleaming work surfaces. She was doing her best to put aside the intensity of the pain that was growing inside her. She would be leaving soon, just as soon as she could throw her things together and get out of this house, and this was probably the last opportunity she would get to talk to the housekeeper face to face. She didn't want to set foot inside Lytham again, and meet the taunting, haunting ghosts of the past.

'If you've no immediate plans I'd like you to stay on and look after the house until everything's settled. I'll be leaving shortly to meet with my stepfather's solicitor.' She had phoned him first thing, at his rooms in Gloucester, and he'd said he could see her any time after four. 'I'd like to be able to tell him you're staying on, and then he'll make arrangements for your wages and the usual bills to be paid out of the estate.'

Mrs Moody, staring at her, wasn't making this easy. Her face had always reminded Georgia of a rat trap. She picked up her faltering voice and stated, 'I won't have any use for Lytham, and eventually it will be sold.'

'I imagined that would be the case.'

Georgia met the unwavering, pebble-like eyes with respect. This elderly woman—had she ever been married, or was 'Mrs' a courtesy title?—was facing redundancy, the loss of her home and very little likelihood of re-employment, all with an icy stoicism that was almost unbelievable. If there was internal, invisible anxiety then Georgia did what she could to relieve it.

'When that happens, you'll be provided with a comfortable pension from my stepfather's estate, enough to retire on. That's one of the things I'll be discussing with the solicitor this afternoon.' And Baines, the gardener. She would make provision for him because Harold hadn't. And then, of course, there was Blossom and Elijah, and the house on Blue Rock island.

Some of the tension that had been holding her spine rigid eased out of the way. She had done what Harold should have done, and didn't expect any thanks or protestations of relieved gratitude. That wasn't Mrs Moody's way. And then the pain started bubbling up to the surface again, barely containable now, the hurt of old betrayal and cruel loss.

She turned to leave, quickly, before she broke down, and the housekeeper said, 'I don't suppose you'll be staying tonight, or coming back.'

Georgia shook her head, unable to speak because the tears she'd mistakenly believed all cried out years ago were threatening to take over again.

'Then I have something for you, if you can spare a few minutes.'

Something for her? Georgia turned, fighting the tight ache in her chest, her throat.

Mrs Moody had never given her so much as a smile in the past. What could she possibly want to give her now? The housekeeper had gone to one of the tall, fitted wall cupboards and was pulling out a chunky cardboard box which she carried to the table.

'When you left home, and stayed with that friend of yours before you went to America, your mother asked me to clear your room. I guessed there'd been a disagreement because I was told to send every single thing you owned to a charity shop.' She ran her work-coarsened hands over the top of the box, then stood back. And stunned Georgia by confiding, 'My husband died before we'd been married a year. We never had a child. But if we had I know I couldn't have wiped it out of my life, no matter what. I thought your mother might relent one day, or, more likely, you might come back, so I put some things aside. Little things. Keepsakes, really.'

Touched more than she could say, Georgia opened the box and found bits of the innocent and gullible creature she had been, slices of the past she had never wanted to see again.

An old exercise book full of romantic twaddle—the vapid love poems written by the child who had imagined herself passionately, eternally in love. Jason's photograph, taken from a family album and put into a silver frame. Her collection of records, sickly sentimental ballads all. A scarf Jason had worn when he'd visited one bitterly cold winter weekend and left behind. It and the photograph had gone with her everywhere—school, Sue's, Lytham.

Other things: books that had been favourites, a few trinkets that her gran had given her—inexpensive, but valuable to Georgia because Gran, at least, had loved her, had given her the pretty, sparkly things when she could afford to. There hadn't been money to spare before her mother had met and married Harold, and by then Gran had been dead for over three years.

'Thank you,' she said. 'It was thoughtful of you.'

The tears she despised but seemed to have no control over brimmed in her eyes. Mrs Moody was no fool; she would have seen the way the plump, graceless teenager had stuck to Jason like a limpet whenever he visited, mooning over him with her silly calf's eyes. And she had saved the pathetic mementoes because maybe there was a closet romantic beneath that grim exterior.

Perhaps the elderly woman half believed that

Jason would see the new slim Georgia in a different light...

In your dreams! If she could remove herself from this house without having to set eyes on him again she would be more than pleased. She'd be ecstatic.

After the last of the guests had departed Jason closed the main door and leant against it. The silence of the house folded around him. Everything had gone smoothly; the only surprise had been Georgia's obvious distress. She'd tried to hide it, but he'd been able to see she was swamped by grief.

Even while his mother had still been alive he'd been aware that Harold strayed. Furtive little affairs—a seventeen-year-old without a brain in her head who'd been hired to give Mrs Moody a hand about the place, the nineteen-year-old daughter of the village publican—always young things, fluff-brained. The list, if he thought about it—and he always tried not to—went on and on. So when Harold had accused Georgia of throwing herself at him he hadn't believed a word of it, had stayed behind to read him the riot act after Georgia had shot out of the room.

But now, for the first time, real doubt had crept in, and he was no longer so sure. She'd corresponded with Harold, met up with him after she'd returned to the UK. He'd left her all his worldly possessions, a very considerable fortune, and her grief today had been real enough to touch.

And he hadn't known the real Georgia back then. While he'd been defending her against Harold's accusations, with Vivienne volubly taking her husband's part, Georgia had been running to her friend, probably already planning an abortion.

The sequence of events ran through his mind like a video tape.

When he'd found the car she'd used had gone he'd guessed she'd gone to Sue's and would be OK. He'd only planned on staying at Lytham a few hours—just long enough to break the news of their marriage arrangements. He'd had to get back to London, to his apartment, to work. He was briefing a barrister early the following morning, for an important case of alleged fraud.

Back at his apartment, he'd phoned Sue's home. Her brother, Guy, had answered. Georgia was with them, asleep in bed, and yes, he'd tell her Jason had called.

He'd spent the next few days trying to contact Georgia, to reassure her that he was there for her and their coming child. But he'd got no reply. Frustrated by his need to be at his office, he'd ended up phoning Vivienne, saying no one was answering at Sue's number.

'Guilty conscience, darling?' she had responded tartly. 'And you sounded so self-righteous when you were calling poor Harold vile names! Georgia phoned me late that night and told me about her pregnancy. If it's true, and frankly I don't give a damn, it proves she came on to Harold, not the other way around as you so nastily suggested. If it is yours, then she must have thrown herself at you, and you didn't display Harold's good sense and tell her to get lost. In any event, the problem needn't give you sleepless nights. It's sorted. She's got rid of it, and you've me to thank for giving her that sound piece of advice.

'You won't be able to reach her. That friend of hers and the brother collected my daughter from a private clinic early this morning and took her off to their holiday beach home to recuperate. As I said, problem sorted, and that's the end of it. I haven't mentioned any of this unsavoury mess to Harold, and I'd be grateful if you never mentioned the little hussy's name in my hearing again.'

He hadn't. He hadn't visited Lytham again, and he had cut Georgia Blake, and what she had done to the child he had surprised himself by wanting so badly, right out of his life, right out of his head.

Until, out of necessity, she'd come back into it.

But it would soon be over, he told himself tightly. He'd just check she intended to speak with Harold's solicitor—he'd given her the telephone number first thing this morning—assure himself that she would make adequate provision for Baines and Mrs Moody, then drive back to London.

He hardened his jaw. He might even contact Sylvia, suggest dinner. They'd been dating, occasionally, for almost a year now. A journalist, forcefully attractive, she was married to her career. They enjoyed each other's company, enjoyed sex, and neither of them was interested in long-term commitments.

Which suited him just fine. He'd lost the inclination, and probably the ability, to get emotionally involved with any woman since—

He strode in the direction of the kitchens. First he'd let Mrs Moody know he was leaving, then find Georgia, say what he had to, and get the hell out.

He met Georgia as she exited the kitchen regions. She was carrying a cardboard box and her face was wet with tears, her eyes huge, tormented, her wide mouth clamped as if she was refusing to let herself speak to him.

He should have said what he wanted to say, then left it, kept everything cool, walked away and made it final.

Instead he found his eyes marking every feature, as if committing it to memory, skimming the glorious tousle of hair that tumbled to her shoulders, the tear-spiked dark lashes that framed those golden eyes, the delicate arch of the cheekbones that had emerged from the roundness of adolescence, the fragile creamy throat rising from the white thing she wore around her neck. Found himself actively pushing contempt into his voice as he slid his hands into his pockets, rocked back on his heels and drawled, 'My goodness, Georgia, you look as if you're mourning a lost and passionately adored lover, not an elderly stepfather you saw just occasionally.'

He really should have left it. He immediately despised himself, as he would despise anyone who was deliberately cruel, wishing the mocking words unsaid as he saw her face crumple, heard the harsh tug of her breath. He began to make an apology but she cut across him.

'You never could see it was all lies, could you? The things Harold said that day.' Her voice was raw with all the pain, the long memory of it. She hated the man in the elegantly tailored dark grey suit, the man with the severe, forbidding face and taunting, merciless eyes.

Hatred and pain spurred her, and she hissed at him, 'Or maybe you just preferred to believe those lies because they gave you a let-out you could take without compromising your notion of bloody duty! You turned your back on me and our baby and thanked your lucky stars you didn't have to marry a fat teenager and make yourself a laughing stock. You didn't care at all.' Her eyes were wide, feral with deep loathing. 'I wanted our baby, more than anything. But you weren't even interested enough to ask what happened then—so why should I bother to explain myself now?' She jerked her head up, pushed past him as he would have detained her. 'You're in my way. I have an appointment in Gloucester.'

She walked stiffly away, controlled, distanced. She had spilled out the pain, told him. Reminded him of how foul he was.

It was the only consolation she had.

Luck was with her, she decided as she put her foot down on the way back to Birmingham. A scant five minutes after that final confrontation with Jason she'd left Lytham without seeing him again. Her meeting with the solicitor had been smooth, and now traffic was light.

And she knew exactly what she was going to do, what she needed. Decorating the apartment, hanging those curtains, fixing shelves could wait.

She would spend the rest of her holiday on Blue Rock, among the Windward Islands in the eastern Caribbean Sea. She would leave the bleak English winter behind, forget the man with the harsh grey eyes, lie on powdery white sand and bake in the sun, swim in crystal blue waters, breathe the scent of oleanders, stuff herself with Blossom's fantastic cooking and rebuild her breached and battered defences.

She was going to the island.

She was going to be all right.

CHAPTER FIVE

THE hot white sand was burning her bottom through her denim shorts. Georgia got to her feet and brushed away the clinging grains. She had been on Blue Rock for three days and had already acquired a light tan.

But nothing else. Certainly not the peace of mind she'd come all the way out here to regain. How could she hope for that when she couldn't get Jason out of her mind? When he walked through her dreams and edged his way into practically every waking thought she had?

She would have been far better off cancelling her leave and getting back to work, she thought with a stab of annoyance. Since she'd hauled herself together, long months after losing her baby, her work and the steep climb up the ladder of promotion had become the most important things in her life, so by throwing herself back on the treadmill she might have found it easier to shut the past right out of her head again.

From the corner of her eye she saw Elijah take the boat out from the small natural harbour at the other end of the sheltered little bay, caught the dull chug of the diesel engine. She lifted a hand to shade her eyes from the glittering light that bounced off the crystal blue waters and wondered whether he was simply out on one of his regular fishing trips or going over to the market on Blue Rock's larger sister island, San Antonio.

Georgia wished she was with him. Either activity would have taken her mind off Jason, and the way seeing him again had affected her, bringing back the pain, as raw and savage as it had ever been.

Following the small boat's progress, she felt the burn of the morning sun on her shoulders and heard Blossom's voice floating down over the low coral cliffs. 'You get right back here, Miss Georgie, and get a hat on that head of yours. You hear me?'

The bossy, stentorian tones broke through her mood, had her turning, acknowledging the instruction with a wave and a wide grin.

Little had changed since she'd visited the island with Harold and her mother, eighteen months after their marriage. Blossom still thought it her duty to order everyone around, 'For their own good', as she righteously termed it, and Elijah, her long-suffering yet devoted husband, still jumped to obey her smallest command. The only difference Georgia could detect was the way Elijah's crinkled hair had turned white and Blossom's ample girth had grown even more ample.

She picked her way back up through the white flowery fronds of frangipani and bougainvillea that hazed the low cliffs, and Blossom said, 'You want to look like a boiled lobster? Get along inside with you. I have an ice-cold lemon drink waiting in the house.'

'You are, as ever, perfectly right,' Georgia conceded. Her face was very straight but her eyes were dancing. If anyone else had spoken to her as if she were a child they would have got the sharp edge of her tongue!

After the snow and ice of England, the Caribbean warmth was fabulous, but in spite of the moderating trade winds the effect of the sun could be fierce. She would slosh on more sunblock and find a shady hat before she went out again.

But Blossom had other ideas.

'You have time to tidy yourself and make a start on sorting through your poor mother's things before your guest arrives. This is your place now; you take charge. It's up to you to do things right. Mr Harold never came back to do these things. Too many bad memories waiting.'

Blossom was already crossing the emerald sward, kept lush and beautiful by Elijah's daily watering, and Georgia caught up with her, frowning. 'Run that past me again, Blossom—I'm not expecting a guest.' The housekeeper must have got her wires crossed somewhere. Either that or she had misheard what had been said.

But there was no mistaking the mild derision in the older woman's dark eyes, the way she turned, planting her hands on her wide hips, scolding, 'Course you are, Miss Georgie. What's got into you, forgetting a thing like that? Mr Jason phoned through from St Vincent a little while ago. The air taxi comes into San Antonio in a coupla hours. Elijah's gone to fetch him back and bring home some good fish.' She turned back to the low, sprawling colonial-style bungalow. 'So, like I just said, you've got time to make yourself respectable and start on your poor mother's room. It isn't proper to leave it, and you surely can't do it while you have Mr Jason to entertain.'

Georgia's blood ran cold, and a frisson of something nameless shot clear through her body. Jason had followed her here, and had obviously led the housekeeper and her caretaker husband to believe he'd been invited. She couldn't understand it.

He'd seemed no more enamoured of her company than she'd been of his. In fact, mutual loathing had produced a crackling tension, practically colouring the air between them while she'd been staying at Lytham.

And she couldn't hop on a bus and get the hell out of here. Getting to and from Blue Rock was a logistical nightmare. So she'd be stuck with him until she could rearrange her return journey for an earlier date.

Stuck, with no place to hide.

Part-way up the shallow flight of steps that led to the deep, shady veranda that skirted the entire building, Georgia stopped, threw back her shoulders and gritted her teeth.

What the hell was the matter with her? The instinct to run and hide from unpleasantness had been the old way, the way of an insecure, too-eager-to-please teenager.

The new rules were very different. She stood her

ground. She could face whatever had to be faced. And that included Jason.

As the De Havilland Twin Otter came in to land Jason looked down into the turquoise-blue waters that surrounded the small island of San Antonio and felt his stomach muscles clench.

Nothing to do with the way the aircraft was banking, the way the tiny airstrip seemed to be leaping towards them. Everything to do with facing Georgia again, facing the past and finally, yes, finally, putting it to rest.

After what she'd said about their baby the instinct to follow her, insist on clearing the air, find out if he shared the blame—if only for believing her to have been more mature than she actually had been at that time—had been utterly compelling.

Maybe if he'd made doubly sure she'd known she had his total and willing support, explained the pole-axing certainty of wanting both her and the child, then she wouldn't have panicked and rushed into an abortion.

But the wanting had been so new to him he'd hardly been able to understand it himself at that time, so how could he have made her understand what he himself had found to be inexplicable?

He knotted his dark brows as the plane taxied slowly towards the hut that passed as an airport terminal, uncomfortable at the rarity of finding he was making excuses for himself.

Besides, there was the other unpalatable aspect. Her relationship with Harold.

When his stepfather had first accused her of throwing herself at him he had dismissed it out of hand. He'd known for years what Harold was like. In any case, it had become a very secondary consideration after he'd learned of her abortion.

To begin with he'd been too angry over the ending of the life that he'd helped to create to trust himself to tackle her about what she'd done, and by the time he'd got his head together it had been too late. Because he'd heard, through Vivienne, that she'd blithely swanned off to the States without, apparently, a single regret, and after that he'd worked hard to put her out of his thoughts.

And had succeeded, until she'd returned to England and Harold had told him of those lunch dates. So what, precisely, had she done to persuade him to leave his entire fortune to her? After seeing this new, sophisticated Georgia, a woman who obviously knew her way around, a woman who positively radiated sex-appeal—and knowing Harold of old—he didn't imagine for a second that there was an innocent explanation.

He unclipped his seat belt and stood up, his mouth grim. He didn't give a damn for Harold's wealth, only the motivation behind his decision. He had come here for one purpose only: to find the truth. The truth about her reasons for the abortion and her real relationship with Harold. Once that was achieved he could lock her away in the past again. And leave her there.

The moment Georgia saw the boat slip round the headland and chug into the bay she let the louvres drop back into place and turned her back on her bedroom window.

She was as ready as she would ever be to face her uninvited, unwanted guest. Across the room she saw herself reflected in the long pier glass. Her slender figure was monotone: narrow oyster-coloured cotton trousers topped by a long-sleeved matching collarless skinny shirt, her mane of hair tamed into a single braid. A deliberate understatement. The only primary colour was the scarlet she'd painted on her mouth. And that was deliberate, too. A single flag of defiance.

She left the room quickly, before Blossom could holler for her to show her face and behave like a proper hostess, her bare feet silent on the cool marble floors. She crossed the main hall area, then moved slowly through the open double doors to stand waiting in the shade of the veranda.

So far and no further.

Once upon a time the merest hint of Jason's arrival in her vicinity would have had her bounding out to meet him, all adoring eyes and a smile wide enough to meet round the back of her head.

Not any more. Never again.

Taking a deep breath of the warm air, heavily perfumed by the flowering vine which coiled exuberantly from one of the glazed earthenware planters, she eased the rigidity from her spine. She had no intention of looking stiffly defensive, as if she had something to hide or be ashamed of. Cool, uninterested should do it.

But when she saw him mount the steps that led up from the natural harbour her stomach twisted over, then tied itself in knots.

He had no right to do this to her, she thought angrily, surreptitiously wiping her suddenly damp palms down the sides of her cotton trousers. She felt nothing for him now, nothing but contempt. She set her teeth, willing her knotted muscles to relax.

Contempt shouldn't make her heart flutter, her mouth go dry.

He was walking with all the remembered looselimbed grace that she'd never seen in any other man, and the ice-green shirt he wore above stylish, beautifully cut fawn chinos did nothing to disguise the strength of the man. And the casual way he hooked the lightweight suit jacket over one shoulder, carrying what appeared to be an overnight bag in his free hand, didn't fool her. There was nothing casual about the cold appraisal of his eyes when he reached her.

She barely registered Elijah's cheery, 'Good mornin', Miss Georgie,' as he carried the cool box full of goodies from San Antonio market round to the back of the building and the kitchen quarters. Registered nothing but a searing sense of intrusion as Jason deliberately held her eyes, invaded her space.

Her nerves had tensed so much she found it impossible to speak. It was up to him to explain his unwanted presence. She jerked her chin up, refusing to let him see that he could affect her in any way at all, except, perhaps, to give her an acute case of terminal boredom!

He regarded her stony expression for long, achingly silent seconds before one dark brow tilted upwards and he condescended to speak. 'Settled in, have you?'

The hint of slightly scornful patronage behind the drawled words loosened her taut vocal cords, but she chose her words carefully, matching his cool drawl.

'Perfectly. Though I won't say I'm pleased to see you. Perhaps you could pander to my curiosity and tell me why you're here.'

To check up on her, quite probably, to make sure she hadn't thrown Blossom and Elijah out on their venerable necks, hadn't invited all her friends along for a monster rave-up. Or merely to make certain, just by his being here, that she didn't enjoy a further second of her time on her island.

A muscle jerked along the hard jawline, the smoke of his eyes turning to slate as he told her heavily, 'To settle the unfinished business between us. It's past time.' Long past time, if he were ever to be allowed to get on with the rest of his life in peace.

Her heart jolted at the implication. She silently, sternly denied it. There was no unfinished business. The slight shrug she gave him was as coolly dismissive as she could make it. 'As far as I'm concerned, any *business* between us—' she emphasised the echo of his words with the sharp touch of ice '—was well and truly finished many years ago.'

But she would never know how he might have countered that statement, because, behind her, Blossom boomed ecstatically, 'Mr Jason! My, you've grown into something mighty special!'

'Blossom!' Overnight bag and jacket discarded, Jason stepped on to the veranda and folded the stout, elderly islander in a bear hug. 'As I was saying to Elijah, it's been a long time.'

'Too long! Why, when your step-daddy first bought this place for your mother—God rest her dear soul—you came two, three times each year. I watched you grow from a young thing—all long skinny arms and legs and enough daredevil mischief to turn my head grey! And now here you is—handsome as the devil himself. How come you don't have a wife and six kids? You tell me that! Now stop squeezing the breath out of my old body and come along in.'

She made a swoop for his discarded belongings, clucking her tongue. 'What's come into you? You were never heedless of your possessions before; that I do vouch for.' She shook the jacket violently, as if to rid it of careless contamination, still smiling besottedly as she led the way into the house. 'Do you still have a taste for old Blossom's chocolate cookies and fresh-made lemonade?'

Jason grinned broadly, responding lightly, 'If it's

all the same to you, I'll settle for a large G and T with plenty—and I do mean plenty—of ice.'

Still grinning, he followed the housekeeper into the cool recesses of the marbled hall, and forgotten, disregarded, Georgia sagged back against one of the supporting columns and folded her lower lip between her teeth. She bit down as hard as she could without actually drawing blood.

She could take being overlooked, left behind like yesterday's newspaper. No problem.

What she couldn't take was the fierce stab of jealousy that had rooted her to the decking when Jason had folded his strong arms around Blossom and greeted her with genuine affection.

She surely hadn't wanted him to greet her that way! If he so much as touched her she would scream with revulsion, she reminded herself.

So why the primeval stab of jealousy?

CHAPTER SIX

IT WASN'T like Georgia to sulk, Jason thought as he stood on the low cliffs and scanned the empty white sands of the sheltered bay. Unless, of course, her character had changed as much as her outward appearance. Which, from his recent encounter with her around Harold's funeral, seemed highly possible.

He'd evaded as many of Blossom's questions—largely to do with his unmarried state—as he decently could, taken his gin and tonic to his room, tossed the meagre contents of his grip into a drawer and gone to look for Georgia.

She'd taken off. He didn't flatter himself that it was because her guilty conscience wouldn't let her face him. This new Georgia acted as if she could outface the Archangel Gabriel if she had to. She'd taken off in a fit of the sulks because his unexpected arrival on the island had given him the upper hand. She would hate that, just about as much as she hated him.

So why was he bothering? he asked himself as he turned towards the thickly treed hills and spurs that formed the interior of the small island. She'd have to put in an appearance some time, and he could have done himself a favour, stayed back at the house, relaxing in the shade, recovering from the journey out that had at times seemed interminable, waiting until she eventually showed her face.

The short answer was that he didn't know. Where she was concerned he felt driven by something beyond sense or reason, beyond control. He was used to being in control and felt edgy, as now, when he wasn't.

A rough path skirted the base of the hills, winding through the suddenly dark green silence of creeper-clad trees. He remembered it well. It led him into the memories of the distant past when Harold, having acquired his second million, had bought the island, a couple of years after Jason's mother had married him. It had been paradise to a boy who had been too young to have lost either innocence or trust.

It also led to the other side of the island, where the woodland almost touched the shore, the trees sheltering swampy ground and the quiet pools where the pond turtles lived.

And she was there, as—instinctively, inexplicably—he had known she would be. He paused, his chest suddenly expanding, as if to accommodate the near painful surge of his heartbeats.

She had her back half turned to him, her bare feet planted in the deep, springy moss as she stared down into the cool depths of one of the larger pools. The plait she'd made of her hair hung forward over one of her slight shoulders, exposing the tender nape of her neck.

A tight ache took his heart and squeezed it. Suddenly, she looked vulnerable again, and very much alone, calling forth the old urge to protect and cherish that had formed the basis of his relationship with her—until that fateful night when, half stupefied by alcohol and fever, stunned by the raw explosion of desire that he had never equated with their relationship before, it had become, without him being fully aware of it, something else entirely.

He didn't want it. He didn't need the painful tug at his heart, the urgent need to hold her in the comfort and safety of his arms. But it held him, despite his mental repudiation, drawing him silently on through the last of the trees to where she stood, lost in thoughts he could only guess at, because for all the entwined strands of the past he had never known her, not truly.

His footfalls had been silenced by the moss, but she showed no surprise when he lightly touched her shoulder, just lifted her head and looked at him, her golden eyes hazed, as if she'd been looking deep into the past, or far into the future—who could tell?

'I think this must be one of the most peaceful spots on earth,' he said quietly, noting the pallor of her skin beneath the recently acquired tan—skin that had the softness and smoothness of rose petals. The vibrant colour of her mouth magnetised his attention, keeping it on the full, sensual curve of her lips.

Just looking at her mouth made him ache right through to his soul. He wanted to take it with his own, feel her lips part for him, inviting him into paradise. She, he was discovering, had the unsettling ability to turn him on more than any other woman.

The knowledge bewildered him, must have fuddled his brain, because he found his hand moving, his fingers untwisting her braided hair, and his bemusement deepened when she didn't object, simply tilted her head slightly towards him, as if to make the task easier.

'I wonder if that's what brought us both here? Because we both felt the need for peace,' she responded thoughtfully, as if the slightly trite remark had struck a chord within her mind.

'It's a fairly elusive commodity,' he concurred softly, his fingers freeing her hair, sensually sliding through the silky strands as if they had taken on an independent life of their own.

He saw her lips part on a gentle sigh, felt the soft flutter of her breath on the triangle of exposed chest where he'd opened his shirt before setting out to look for her, and felt himself slipping into uncharted territory, as if his mind had become utterly divorced from reality.

Weakly, Georgia lowered her eyes and gazed down into the dark, translucent depths of pool. Unable to follow the other two, to listen to Blossom's endless chatter, she'd walked away from the house like a robot, her feet unwittingly bringing her to this secluded, tranquil spot. Where she'd waited. Because some deep, primeval instinct had told her he would come. Because it was fated.

What had he said? *Unfinished business.*

In some strange way the inevitability of it had relaxed her, so that by the time he had come to her she was in a state of what she could only muzzily assume was trance. And the closeness of his hard male body, the musky, slightly sharp scent of him, the intimate haze of his body heat and the stroke and slide of his fingers through her hair released the last vestige of tightness in her mind, freed her to submerge herself in every insidious sensation.

Sternly forbidden for so long, it all came back in swamping waves of hedonistic pleasure. The meltdown of her bones, the headlong rush of fire through her veins, the pooling of liquid heat deep inside her. So long forgotten, yet so easily remembered.

She swayed towards him, languid, lost, her legs buckling beneath her, and his arms folded around her as he eased them both to the cool, mossy ground.

'This heat,' he muttered thickly. 'You're not used to it.'

'And you are?' She was teasing, gently mocking his unconscious male superiority, but her voice came thickly, the words spaced out and slow, as if she were drugged. She felt drugged. She sought his eyes. They were smoky with what seemed to be happening here, his brow slightly furrowed as if he, too, were grasping for the reality that was endlessly receding.

'I can take it.' His lids lowered heavily, his lashes thick dark crescents against the olive tones of his moisture-slicked skin, his eyes lingering on her mouth, at last to move on to slide down the fragile length of her neck, down to the uncompromising armour of her long-sleeved shirt, to swing up again and lock with the bemused golden light of hers.

'So buttoned up. No wonder the heat's getting to you.' It was an excuse, and he knew it, and wondered if she knew it, too. An excuse to allow the tips of his fingers to ease the rigid row of buttons from their fastenings. An excuse to devour her body with his eyes, to touch the inviting creamy flesh.

When the last button was free of its moorings he eased her on to her back, met no resistance, felt the powerful surge of his manhood with a stab of wild, head-spinning elation, knew without doubt that she was his.

As she had been his on that one earth-shattering night, when his perceptions of himself, of her, had changed beyond recognition.

And his life had changed thereafter, that strand of bitterness had been introduced into his heart and soul, the voice of sanity reminded him. A voice that was lost when her lips parted on a husky whimper of helpless capitulation and she wound her arms around his neck, urged his head down to the pouting globes of her naked breasts.

He needed no further invitation to turn the tortured dreams of the last seven years into ecstatic reality. Hungrily, he took each erect peak in turn as her body arched and writhed beneath him.

His hands found the zip at the front of her trousers and dragged it down, and the blood pounded hotly through his veins, throbbing wildly at his temples, as she lifted her hips to allow him to slide the light fabric down, to allow him access to the warm, softly furred mound of her femininity.

The sensuality of her movements blew his mind, and he fought the primitive instinct to simply take her. He had to cool it, find control, make this slow and perfect for her. For both of them. Make it as it should be.

He shuddered, and saw her soft mouth tremble, saw the glitter of gold beneath her lowered eyelids and bent his head again, to trail tender kisses down to her navel, then back again, to the temptation of her creamy breasts, slowing it down, fighting back the urgency, easing her now wild and glorious hair to cover the pert globes, kissing them through the soft, silky veil.

Against his intentions, the gentle teasing appeared to drive her wild, inciting her to wind those slenderly elegant legs tightly around his body, opening for him, her voice raw with passion, thick and heady with it as she cried out his name.

His voice shaky with the effort of holding back, he said, 'Such beautiful hair—it always was soft and silky, now it's so long, and full of glorious light. Whatever you do to it, it's inspired.'

She'd been lost, drugged by sensation, entrapped by memories of loving him, the yearning and passion that had blossomed for him, and only him. Lost in it all. But not now. Now she found herself—the woman she had become, not the simple girl she had been, the girl who had been so betrayed.

Memories changed abruptly. A crystal-clear flashback of Sue, dragging her off to a top New York stylist, telling her it was past time she took some interest in her appearance. It had been six months since she'd lost her baby. She had to start living again.

The stylist had transformed the long, unkempt mass, not losing the length, but cleverly shaping and layering it to give style and life, brightening the mousy-brown with what had seemed like a trillion fine blonde highlights.

The new, flattering hairstyle, coupled with her weight loss, had marked the beginning of her new attitude. Become part of her persona, her life. As Jason wasn't, and never could be.

With a smothered cry of anguish she pressed the palms of her small hands against his shoulders and pushed him away, frantically scrabbling to cover herself.

'Just leave me alone!' she commanded tightly, dragging the edges of her shirt together. 'I didn't ask you to come here. I don't want you here.'

She saw the flare of his nostrils, the white line of what was probably temper appear around his mouth, and it incensed her. He looked like a man who had been deprived of something he believed he had a right to take!

Pushing the shirt into the waistband of her hastily pulled-up trousers, her hands shaking with rage, shoving her feet into the sturdy slip-ons she'd discarded so she could feel the soft coolness of the moss beneath her feet, she stated rigidly, 'Don't ever try to touch me again. You caught me when my guard was down—what's your excuse?'

Jason got slowly to his feet, dragging a long-fingered hand over his tight jawline as he felt the savage ache of frustrated need ebb as quickly as it had flowed, the shock of her explosive rejection suddenly clearing his head. He couldn't excuse what had happened between them because he sure as hell couldn't understand it.

'I didn't think I needed one. It's not the first time you've thrown yourself at me, remember? You seem to make a habit of it,' he added drily. Tousled hair, her golden eyes ablaze with anger, she looked magnificent, wild and incredibly sexy.

He fought back the hot, resurgent stab of need the only way he knew how, employing the first weapon to come to hand, using the thought that had lurked at the back of his mind since his stepfather's death. 'I can't imagine you leading Harold on, then giving him a similar slap in the face. Because as sure as God made little green apples he wouldn't have left his entire fortune to you if you had.'

The utter hatefulness of his taunt was a pain that had no ending. It would have had her on her knees, sobbing her heart out, if she'd let it, the pain of knowing he had always believed what Harold had said all those years ago, his belief reinforced by the contents of that will.

Retaining the pain within her rigidly held body, not letting him guess at his power to hurt her, she raised one finely arched brow in his direction. 'How very astute you've become, Jason. I guess it must come with the job.' And she swept past him, heading for the path between the trees. She wasn't going to argue with him. He could think what he damned well liked.

'I shan't want anything, Blossom. I've got a raging headache, so I'll turn in and have an early night.'

It wasn't a lie. Her head felt as if it were about to split in two. But nothing short of her immediate demise would obliterate the housekeeper's notion of what was right and what was wrong.

'You can do no such thing, Miss Georgie! Whatever would Mr Jason think? His first night here, too!'

Blossom had been preparing peppered shrimps for the supper Georgia had no intention of sharing with Jason, and now she wiped her hands on her huge white coverall and plonked them on her hips, repeating, 'Whatever would he think of your manners?'

Georgia couldn't care less. 'I'm sure he'll understand, if you explain it to him nicely.' She crossed to the fridge and poured herself a glass of juice. The sun had set in a blaze of gold and crimson, dropping swiftly through the dark blue sky. Now she could see fireflies dancing giddily through the wide uncurtained kitchen windows.

She had no idea if Jason had returned to the bungalow or been caught in the quickness of the Caribbean nightfall. And didn't want to know.

Disregarding Blossom's objections, she went to her room and closed the door firmly behind her. She was fond of the older woman, had come to terms with her idiosyncrasies during the weeks she'd spent here all those years ago, and remembered her with affection. But the housekeeper was going to have to learn that Little Miss Georgie had grown up, developed a mind of her own!

She had even, before Jason had appeared and ruined the tranquillity, decided to keep the island, to visit as often as she could, offer it as a holiday opportunity for her friends and colleagues. Blossom and Elijah would love having people to look after.

But Jason's unexpected arrival had tainted the place, spoiled everything. He was the serpent in this paradise. She didn't think she would ever want to set foot on the island again.

The sleep she craved eluded her. When the illuminated dial of the bedside clock showed two a.m. she gave up, pulled on a short silky robe and padded out of the room.

At the far end of the wide, marble-floored corridor she took a deep breath to steady herself, and opened the door to the master suite. At least Blossom would applaud the fact that she'd at last psyched herself up to sort through the things Vivienne had left behind when she'd fled the island all those years ago.

Wide awake and fully alert, Jason heard doors open and close. So Georgia couldn't sleep, either. Were the memories of what had happened between them earlier keeping her awake, too?

He would have liked to blame his sleepless state on the peppered prawns, the pumpkin pie and home-made ice-cream Blossom had served him. But in all honesty couldn't.

Not wanting to eat a thing, he'd forced himself to for the housekeeper's sake. She'd been miffed enough about Georgia's refusal of supper.

'Miss Georgie says sorry, but she's got herself a big headache. She's gone to bed to sleep it off. She don't heed what I say—goes out in the sun without her hat—I worry my head about her.'

'Don't.' He'd eyed the fancily laid table, the great quantities of rich food with a desperation he'd been doing his best to hide. 'Miss Georgie's all grown up now; she can look after herself.'

And wasn't that the truth! She'd latched on to Harold's weakness for pretty young things and feathered her nest very nicely, thank you! And, this afternoon, had had no qualms about as good as admitting it!

It sickened him to his soul. He wanted to walk away from the hard-nosed, sophisticated little madam she'd become and forget she'd ever existed.

But he couldn't. Not until she'd fully explained what had happened to their baby. Not knowing was his private demon. A demon that wouldn't let him rest.

He'd fouled up this afternoon. His intention had been to talk, to begin to sort out their unfinished business, and he'd ended up touching her, wanting her with a force that had blown his mind.

It wouldn't happen again. Forewarned of the crazy

effect she could have on him, he'd make absolutely certain it didn't!

Swinging his legs out of bed, he strode to the *en suite* bathroom to cover his naked body with the towelling robe that was hanging on the back of the door, and let himself out into the corridor.

Blossom and Elijah's quarters were in the annexe, so Georgia had to be the nocturnal wanderer. He'd track her down and insist they had the talk that was overdue by seven years.

At the end of the corridor a strip of light showed beneath the master suite door. He walked towards it. His heart was thumping loudly in his chest. He ignored it and pushed open the door.

CHAPTER SEVEN

A SINGLE lamp illuminated the top of the delicate writing desk she was sitting at. Jason spared a single, impatient glance at the rest of the dimly lit master bedroom, noted the jewel colours of the clothes that had been neatly folded and stacked on the ice-blue satin bedspread, but his eyes were immediately drawn back again to the scarlet-robed figure immobile in the pool of light.

She had scooped her hair up on top of her head, revealing her long, elegant neck, and the droop of her slender shoulders as her fingers smoothed the surface of the handwritten sheet of paper in front of her gave her an almost childlike vulnerability that jerked at his heartstrings.

Coupled with the in-your-face sensuality of the body so carelessly covered by a slick of scarlet silk, it was a combination that threatened to destroy his intention to keep the hoped-for conclusion of business between them civilised and cool.

A frown drew his brow down above his narrowed eyes. She couldn't have failed to hear him come into the room, and yet she didn't turn to face him, didn't move a muscle apart from the slow slide of her fingers over the sheet of paper.

'Georgia! Can we talk?' He regretted the involuntary harshness of his voice, regretted it more when, with every appearance of deep reluctance, she turned to him and he saw her face. It was wet with tears, and the brilliance of her eyes was dulled by a deep inner anguish that made his breath catch in his throat.

The desire to go to her, to hold her, comfort her, was strong enough to make him shake. He denied the impulse firmly. Getting close to her was dangerous. He didn't need reminding of the mindless mistake he'd made earlier in the day.

He stuffed his hands in the pockets of the robe he was wearing and said as impartially as he could, 'Something's obviously troubling you. Want to talk about it? Or wouldn't that help?'

Georgia swallowed painfully; she was beyond coherent speech. If she tried to get one word out past the hot, aching constriction in her throat she would break down in sobs and humiliate herself. She'd done enough of that this afternoon.

Besides, the letter she'd discovered in the desk drawer and had only just finished reading when he'd walked in had knocked the stuffing clean out of her. For the moment she had nothing to fight him with.

Wordlessly, she held out the paper, and he took it, distancing himself, though, going to the other side of the room and leaning against the ornately carved footboard of the bed. The frown line between his eyes deepened as he read. Though whether that was down to the dimness of the light on that side of the room or the contents of the letter, she didn't know.

The contents. Already the words were branded on her brain.

> My dear Georgia,
> I'm writing because I haven't the courage to phone and beg for a face-to-face meeting. I have so much to apologise for. For treating you shamefully since your birth, for not being able to love you as a mother should. For refusing to have you back at Lytham. The list goes on—
>
> Is it too much to ask that we meet and try to build bridges? I know I don't have the right to ask anything of you. But it would mean so much to me. And perhaps mean something to you.

There was no more. Vivienne hadn't finished writing the letter before something had made her leave Blue Rock so precipitately. And she had been killed in her car before she'd had time to write again.

Georgia watched Jason walk slowly back to her side, his tall, lean body dominating her, the intense sexual awareness making her heart turn over.

She didn't want it, didn't need it. Couldn't cope with the basic instinct that had been with her since her teens. The only way she could handle it was by making him her enemy, fighting him.

She'd stopped fighting him this afternoon, and just look at what had happened!

Since reading the unfinished letter the fight had gone out of her, so perhaps he'd do the decent thing and leave her to mourn the loss of the reconciliation her mother had wanted, lost because she'd run out of time.

But he didn't, simply lowered her defences to zero when he said compassionately, his dark, soft voice sending shivers down the length of her spine, 'At least you have the comfort of knowing that your mother wanted to make amends.'

She dipped her head, afraid of baring raw emotion in front of him, but he tilted her head up with one finger, just under her chin, and she was forced to witness the smoky compassion in his eyes as he told her, 'I knew, from the moment she came into Harold's life, that she had little time for you. It used to cut me up, seeing your insecurities. I put her behaviour down to a rather selfish woman's absorption in her new marriage, a new and wealthy lifestyle. But there was obviously more. It went way back to your birth. Can you tell me more? I'm not prying, but it might help to lay a few ghosts.'

In this gentler, more receptive mood he was doubly dangerous. The basic instinct to love this man, the blistering sexual chemistry between them, the tenderness... Right at this moment she was too weakened to resist.

'Perhaps,' she conceded, and slid the letter back into the drawer. She would take it with her when she went. Not the designer clothes her mother had adored, nor the jewellery she'd left behind. Just the letter. Because there, at last, was her means of forgiving the past.

'Not here.' He stepped back a pace as she stood up, careful not to touch her, but his eyes were kind.

She mentally excused her meek compliance. Perhaps that was what she needed right now. Perhaps kindness from the man who had betrayed her, turned his back on her when she'd so badly needed him, would help her recover from the shock of finding that letter.

She needed to know that he was capable of having consideration for her, benevolent feelings. It would help her to know that the love of her young life hadn't been wasted on a heart that was completely black, just as she was beginning to understand that her mother hadn't meant it, not deep down, when she'd said she never wanted to see her daughter again.

Passing the back of her hand over her still aching forehead, she followed him from the room, and he told her, 'We could both use something to relax us, I guess. Hot milk and whisky should do the trick.' He could do with a stiffener, but her need looked greater than his. The dark rings around her eyes, the tight cast of her features, made her look brittle—as if, carelessly handled, she could break into a million pieces.

He pushed open the kitchen door and leaned in to flick on the lights, waiting for her to precede him. Almost as though, Georgia thought, he wanted her under his eye, to make sure she didn't run and hide.

Entering the room ahead of him, she made for the cane two-seater against the far wall, sinking down on to the squashy cushions where Blossom took her 'little breathers'.

Her adrenalin supplies had all dried up, she decided as she watched him pour milk into the pan he'd selected, then slosh what looked like a suspiciously huge amount of spirit into two earthenware mugs. No sign of the primitive urge to flee or fight.

His back to her, he remarked, 'You've only visited the island once before, as I recall. Eighteen months or so after Vivienne married Harold.'

The unfinished business between them would have to wait; he wanted to get her talking about her mother because, whether she knew it or not, she needed to. His gut instinct to care for her didn't surprise him. It had always been there, ever since their first meeting. In spite of everything, the need to protect her surfaced naturally now, as if it had been programmed into him.

He handed her the mug of hot, whisky-laced milk and perched at the end of Blossom's sofa, his own mug cradled in his hands, knowing he had to be careful not to appear to pressure her.

Georgia nodded, taking a tentative sip of the hot drink. The combination had sounded pretty unpalatable to her, but the hot creamy milk took the fire out of the spirit and went down easily. Leaning back against the cushions, she told him, 'After that first time, they never brought me back. As you know, I usually spent the long summer holidays between Sue and her family and Lytham. But Mother loved this place. They came often.'

'What did you do? Blot your copybook?' he asked lightly. There was a speck of creamy milk on her upper lip. The tip of her tongue peeped out to capture it. He looked away quickly, tightening his mouth as desire stabbed with wicked ferocity inside him, and heard her answer, sounding much more relaxed now.

'I don't think so. They weren't around enough to get fed up with me. Harold used to hire a motor launch so they could visit San Antonio whenever they wanted, without having to rely on Elijah. I stayed here—swimming, exploring the island, going fishing with Elijah and being fussed over or bossed around by Blossom. I had a whale of a time.'

The only thing she'd longed for was for Jason to put in an appearance; she'd missed not seeing him once during the five weeks she'd spent here.

She drained the last drop from her mug. Better not to think of that old infatuation. She could think of it and deride herself for it when he was back to being her enemy again. 'Mother much preferred San Antonio—it has great shops, apparently, a couple of superb restaurants and plenty of sophisticated nightlife.'

I just bet she did, Jason thought acidly. Vivienne

MILLS & BOON®

An Important Message from The Editors of Mills & Boon®

Dear Reader,

Because you've chosen to read one of our romance novels, we'd like to say "thank you"!

And, as a **special way** to thank you, we've selected <u>four more</u> of the <u>books</u> you love so much **and** a welcome gift to send you absolutely <u>FREE!</u>

Please enjoy them with our compliments...

Tessa Shapcott

Editor, Mills & Boon

P.S. And because we value our customers we've attached something extra inside...

PEEL OFF AND PLACE INSIDE

MILLS & BOON®

With our compliments

THE EDITORS

alidate your ... ift "Thank You"

e Gift Seal from the front
ace provided to the right.
s you to receive four free
oldtone book locket.

details on the card,
line, and post it back to
Ve'll then send you four
the Presents...™ series.
il value

ur satisfaction is guaranteed
ou're under no obligation to buy
ything. We charge you nothing for
ur introductory parcel. And you
on't have to make any minimum
number of purchases – not even
one! Thousands of readers
have already discovered that
the Reader Service is the
most convenient way of
enjoying the latest new romance
novels before they are available
the shops. Of course, postage and
packing is completely FREE.

Tessa Shapcott
Editor, Mills & Boon

r complimentary book m

Yours FREE...
when you reply today

This delicate book locket is a necklace with a difference... The hinged book is decorated with a romantic floral motive and opens to reveal two oval frames for your most cherished photographs. Respond today and it's yours free.

Yes! Please send me my four FREE books and a welcome gift

PLACE FREE GIFT SEAL HERE

Yes! I have placed my free gift seal in the space provided above. Please send me my four free books along with my welcome gift. I understand I am under no obligation to purchase any books, as explained on the back and opposite page. I am over 18 years of age.

P9HI

Surname (Mrs/Ms/Miss/Mr) _____ Initials_____

Address _____

_____

_____

_____ Postcode _____

Offer valid in the UK only and not valid to current subscribers to the Presents... series. Overseas readers please write for details. We reserve the right to refuse an application and applicants must be aged 18 years or over. Only one application per household. Terms and prices subject to change.

As a result of this application you may receive further offers from Harlequin Mills & Boon Limited and other carefully selected companies. If you do not want to share in this opportunity, please write to the Data Manager at the address overleaf. Offer expires 29th February 2000.

Mills & Boon is a registered trademark owned by Harlequin Mills & Boon Limited.

Presents... is being used as a trademark.

◄ Detach along the dotted line and post this card today. No stamp needed

HOW THE READER SERVICE WORKS

Accepting the free books places you under no obligation to buy anything. You may keep the books and gift and return the despatch note marked "cancel". If we don't hear from you, about a month later we will send you 6 brand new books and invoice you for only £2.40* each. That's the complete price – there is no extra charge for postage and packing. You may cancel at any time, otherwise every month we'll send you 6 more books, which you may either purchase or return – the choice is yours.

*Terms and prices subject to change without notice.

The Reader Service™
FREEPOST CN81
CROYDON
CR9 3WZ

NO STAMP NEEDED

had loved the high life, going places where she could be seen in all that expensive designer gear. Blue Rock would have simply been a convenient base from which to visit the exclusive playground of the larger island, where the ordinary residents didn't go because no way could they have afforded the mile-high prices.

But he held his tongue, because now he had Georgia in a relaxed mood he didn't want to ruin it. Not yet, anyway. Not until he found the right moment to bring up the subject of the abortion.

'You say "apparently". Didn't you go there?'

She shook her head and a few soft tendrils dropped from the loose knot on top of her head to frame her face. 'Only passing through, from the airstrip to the quayside.'

That figured. Vivienne wouldn't have wanted to be seen with the awkward, painfully shy sixteen-year-old Georgia would have been at that time. It wouldn't have suited the image she'd created for herself.

Yet there was more to it than that. The letter had revealed that Vivienne had never really loved her daughter. He took their empty mugs and rinsed them at the stainless steel double sink, carefully keeping his back to her, his tone as casual as he could make it as he asked, 'Were the two of you ever close?'

Vaguely, she wondered whether to give him the short answer, and then decided against it. She had always found him easy to talk to. And, in the light of her mother's final wish to get closer to her at last, she needed to get their relationship in perspective, see it from all angles.

'Never. She resented me. But you have to understand why,' she told him thoughtfully, noting the dark frown as he turned back to face her. 'I don't know what she told Harold—we never shared confidences—but she got pregnant with me not long after she left school. She and my father—and don't ask, because she never even told me his name—were engaged, going to be married. But he did a runner when he found out I was on the way. Whether he was frightened off because he couldn't face the idea of fatherhood, or whether the promise of marriage had been a ploy to get her in bed, who can tell?'

She shrugged. It was of no importance now. Aware that Jason was about to rejoin her on the sofa, she shifted slightly to make more space, quickly twitching the edges of her robe together.

'So?' he prompted, noting that her attempt at modesty did nothing to disguise the fact that she was naked beneath the wispy silk, noting his own body's immediate reaction and quietly despairing of himself.

'So she was left, literally, holding the baby. I think Gran would have disowned her if she'd got rid of me or put me up for adoption. She had rigid principles, of the "You've made your bed, now you must lie in it" sort. Money was tight, so from what I gathered Vivienne settled down to get the secretarial skills she needed to support us all while Gran looked after me.'

'It's not a unique story,' he put in, unable to stop himself. It didn't excuse subjecting an innocent child to a life without love. That posthumous letter, the olive branch, was making Georgia defend and excuse her mother.

Almost as if she hadn't registered his comment, she said slowly, as if working it out for herself was something she had to do, 'Then Gran got ill. My mother signed on at an agency, took temporary jobs so she could work around having to look after the two of us, me and Gran. She was still young, and very pretty, and she wanted what she couldn't have—fun, nice clothes to wear when she wasn't working, a life of her own. I once overheard her telling Gran, "I'm stuck with it—what kind of future can I expect? What man would want me, saddled with this wretched child?" But in the end it did work out, because she met Harold, and when he proposed she must have thought all her Christmases had come at once.'

But it hadn't altered her attitude to her child, Jason reflected. Resentment and spite were all Vivienne had ever offered her daughter. He would never forget the malice in her voice when she'd informed him over the phone of Georgia's abortion.

Why? Had she been viciously glad that her daughter would never have what she herself had lacked: not just a child—Vivienne had a child—

but a child she could love and cherish? And the Georgia who had told him of her pregnancy, who had listened to the plans he'd laid out for their wedding, would have loved their child. He would stake his life on that.

So what had happened in such a short space of time to change her mind?

He gave her a fleeting glance. Now was the time to find out.

But she forestalled him. 'I've been wondering why she left this place in such a hurry. It wasn't like her to leave so many lovely things behind.'

'Because she discovered Harold having a furtive fumble with a little waitress on San Antonio. She actually witnessed it, apparently, which meant she couldn't pretend it hadn't happened,' he clipped, deliberately crude. Her admission earlier today of her relationship with Harold—or yesterday, as it now was—had come back to him, igniting the sickening slow burn of anger inside him.

He got to his feet, unable to sit still a second longer. He needed to let her know what type of man she'd got involved with when she'd decided to play her stepfather for all she could get.

'It was an addiction. Silly young girls. Just a bit of fun, nothing serious—that was his excuse.' Bitterness broke into his voice. He let it stay there. 'I'm damned sure, with hindsight, he broke my mother's heart. And ultimately he drove Vivienne to her death. She left the island, fortuitously in time to hop on an airbus, got back to the UK, to Lytham, got in her car and simply drove away. One of the locals said she was driving like a maniac. The rest you know.'

He strode to the door, opened it, turned to face her. But he directed his gaze to a foot above her head. He couldn't meet her eyes, afraid of the knowing indifference he might see there. Perhaps she had known what the man was like but had been too avaricious to care.

'An illness in childhood meant Harold could never father a child, which is why, both times he married, he picked out a woman who already had a child of her own. It's a pity Vivienne didn't have a son, rather than a daughter. To give him his due, he wasn't interested in teenage lads.'

Turning abruptly, he told her, 'Better get back to bed for what's left of the night.'

He'd promised himself he'd get to the truth about her reasons for aborting their child, but the opportunity had passed. He felt too sickeningly angry over her muddy relationship with Harold to handle the conversation with the tact and patience he knew would be called for.

Tomorrow, he thought, flinging himself face-down on the bed, he would have calmed down enough to talk to her rationally, get the truth and leave.

Georgia woke at midday, but only because Blossom came into the bedroom with a tray of fresh fruit and steaming hot coffee.

The housekeeper opened the shutters and let the bright light in, washing the cool lemon walls with gold. 'Has that headache gone? Mr Jason said to leave you to sleep, but I thought you needed some food inside you; 'specially since you didn't eat supper.'

Georgia blinked. Even Blossom's most solicitous whisper was loud! 'I'm fine, now, thank you.' She pulled herself up against the pillows to accept the tray, aware that she'd fallen into bed still wearing the scarlet robe. The dose of whisky Jason had put into her hot milk must have been of knock-out proportions.

Thinking of him injected that familiar squirming, tightening sensation deep inside her. She wished her stupid body would grow some sense, stop responding so catastrophically to him. No other man could do that to her. And more than a few had tried.

Hoping her face hadn't gone as red as she felt it had, she dug the spoon into the bowl of diced fruit. Inwardly deploring her need to know, and trying to sound off-hand, she asked, 'What's Jason doing?'

'Gone fishin' with Elijah. Let's hope it improves his bad temper!'

'Bad temper?' What had brought that on? Last night—despite the strange madness that had overtaken them both in the afternoon, and to which, thankfully, he hadn't referred—he had shown her nothing but consideration, offering her the release of talking about her early years with a mother who had never wanted her. Only when he'd spoken of Harold's serial philandering had his voice grown harsh, and that was understandable, considering what his mother must have had to endure.

'Bad mood, more like,' Blossom amended. 'Like a black crow sitting on his shoulders! Why want to be like that on such a lovely day?'

Why, indeed? Georgia thought as Blossom left her to finish her belated breakfast in peace. Pouring herself a second cup of coffee, she decided she wasn't going to let it bother her. After last night there was too much to think about, so today, with Jason safely out of the way, she would just go with the flow, relax, enjoy all that this small slice of paradise could offer.

After her shower she got into her one-piece swimsuit. The amber colour matched her eyes— eyes which seemed oddly wide and innocent this morning.

Pushing her feet into canvas slip-ons, and cramming a floppy-brimmed straw hat on her head, she reflected that she seemed to have left her sharp, street-wise persona back in the coldness of the English winter.

It didn't bother her. She'd get it all back, no question, as soon as she returned home and took up the threads of her real life again. Then, as she was stuffing her tube of sunblock, her sunglasses and a fat paperback into a flowery cotton shoulder bag, she wondered if this relaxed, go-with-the-flow mood was down to island magic or Jason's presence.

The island, of course. She dismissed the other possibility out of hand as being utter nonsense. She was feeling good despite his presence, not because of it! And she needn't give him a second thought, because he was out fishing, bad mood and all. He could keep his bad mood to himself!

The water was perfect. After a few lazily executed breaststrokes Georgia turned on her back and floated, allowing her mind to drift around the sensation of being naked in the gently moving, warm, crystal-clear salt water of the isolated cove.

It was, she decided, a very, very sensual experience. She'd heard that skinny-dipping was something else, and so hadn't quashed the sudden impulse to strip out of her swimsuit when she'd reached the water's edge.

This was a private island and no one came here. Jason and Elijah were well out of the way, somewhere in the open seas, and if Blossom came down to the shoreline and hollered at her to, 'Get right back here this minute, Miss Georgie, and make yourself respectable!' she'd ignore her, pretend she hadn't heard.

But all she could hear was the gentle lapping of the wavelets on the white, hot sand, birdsong from the forest that clothed the hills... And then, terrifyingly, the total disruption of the water beside her, the splash of dozens of cascading waterfalls.

She twisted frantically, her heart pumping, because surely to goodness some great fish was about to swallow her whole, and found herself staring into something far more dangerous.

Jason's eyes.

CHAPTER EIGHT

THE fishing trip hadn't worked. He'd hoped that going out in the boat, listening to the lazy, hypnotic slap of the water against the hull, to Elijah's slow drawl as he recounted local gossip gleaned on the larger sister island, would have eased the black demon from his back.

If anything, the restricted confines of the small vessel had made him even edgier. And when Elijah had pulled in the rods and announced that they might as well go out beyond the headland, to more productive fishing grounds, he'd cried off, stripping down to his black swimming briefs and diving off the stern of the boat into the sheltered blue crystal waters.

He knew very well what was bugging him. That unfinished business with Georgia. Bobbing about in a boat on the Caribbean Sea, waiting for fish to bite, wasn't going to give him the answers he needed.

And, dammit all, that was what he'd come for. Answers. Nothing else.

A fast crawl for the first few hundred metres had unknotted tense muscles, stretched them, soothed away some of the tension that had been a tight band inside his head since he'd woken at daybreak.

The shoreline of Blue Rock's secluded cove well

in sight, he'd eased off the punishing pace, settled into a leisurely side-stroke, and firmly reminded himself that what Georgia had done to earn her inheritance didn't matter at all to him.

She hadn't blinked so much as an eyelash when he'd spelled out exactly the type of man Harold had been. She obviously hadn't cared, so long as the pickings were rich enough.

Well, she was more than welcome to the lot. He wasn't and never had been, interested in his stepfather's fortune. And he definitely didn't care what she did in her private life. The guy who'd answered her number on his third or fourth attempt to contact her after she'd left Lytham was the same guy who'd answered when he'd phoned her that first time, to let her know the time of Harold's funeral. He'd recognised the voice.

Obviously he was her current live-in lover. He'd certainly sounded pretty sour when he'd given Jason the information that Georgia had left that morning for her island in the sun. In a strop because they were a couple and he hadn't been invited along?

Whatever. It wasn't any of his business. The only thing he was interested in was her reason for aborting their child. For seven years he'd believed he'd managed to put the anger behind him, forget it, forget her. But meeting her again had brought it bubbling back to the surface, and he couldn't get it out of his head.

He only missed colliding with her because he'd

neared the shoreline and decided to wade back through the chest-high water.

She was floating on her back, the silky soft nakedness of her open to his eyes. With a ragged gasp that stopped his heartbeats he took in the sheer beauty of her body, the provocative sexiness of the pert breasts tilted towards the blue sky, hair streaming around her head like a fantastic species of seaweed, the tiny span of her waist and delicately curved tummy, the long and lovely legs slightly parted.

With another ragged gasp his heart thundered on, and he was floundering, struggling to get his footing, because the tempting loveliness of her had made him giddy with raw, primitive desire.

Another flurry of water, thrashing the satiny surface to a white-lace foam, and she was twisting around with the litheness of a mermaid, the evident fright in her wide golden eyes deepening and sharpening as they locked with his.

Tense expectancy danced between them, as sharp and as brilliant as the sunlight glittering on the sea. It locked the air in his lungs, his voice in his throat. His eyes were drawn to her; he wanted to feast on her beauty, ached to touch her, possess her. Touch and possess every bewitching inch of her.

Briefly closing his eyes, he hauled himself together. He would not be led down that road again, no matter how hard he was tempted.

'Sorry if I startled you.' He was the one to find his voice first. Was relieved to find it creditably normal. She was still looking as if a bomb had just exploded in her vicinity.

He found his footing on the sandy bottom, slicked wet hair back off his face and suggested evenly, 'Time we both got out of the water, got covered up before we burn,' and waded back towards the shore, wryly aware of the hollowness of his words.

He was already burning. Burning for that delectable body. And he had nothing to cover up with. Of necessity he'd left his denim cut-offs and T-shirt back in the boat.

Thankfully, though, his body's automatic response to the unexpected, glorious nakedness of her was back under control. She was behind him, probably reluctantly following his advice, seeing the sense of protecting her skin from the sun. Regretting her naked state? Or did the little witch enjoy driving men mad? Did she revel in the power she had?

Too late for modesty now, though she probably wouldn't see it that way. He found her abandoned swimsuit and turned briefly to toss it to her.

She caught it deftly, but before she clutched it to her body he saw the sunlight glitter on the myriad droplets of water that spangled her skin.

Battening down the driving urge to follow the tracks of each and every one of those droplets with his lips, his tongue, his hands, he turned his back to her and said, 'I've got something to ask you, and it's important.' His voice sounded raw. 'We'll talk over there, in the shade.'

There was a gaily patterned umbrella erected near

the low cliffs. He headed for it, collecting her beach bag and canvas slip-ons as he went. No towel. She wouldn't have seen the need for one, so near to the house. Pity. He could have spread it over his lap.

But thinking of the abortion, keeping his mind exclusively on that, should put a dampener on any wayward designs his body might have.

The black swimming trunks he was wearing were disgracefully brief, Georgia thought with a tinge of annoyance as she padded over the hot sand behind him. No man had the right to look so sinfully sexy. The sun-kissed tan of his skin was sleek over hard muscle and bone: wide, rangy shoulders, broad, sinewy back tapering down to that hard, flat waist, mean and moody hips and long, long strong legs.

It was too much! She tried to keep her eyes pinned anywhere but on him, but they seemed to have taken on a will of their own and kept winging back to him.

Sighing, she followed to where he'd settled in the shade. She'd scrambled into her swimsuit, wondering how much of her nakedness the water had hidden from his eyes and deciding that she'd be better off not coming up with the answer to that.

'What is it you want to ask?' The swimsuit, which had seemed so ordinary when she'd put it on, now felt too high-cut on her hip bone, the neckline too low, the whole thing too revealing. She hovered, wanting to take flight. But he had said it was important. Probably something to do with her inheritance. 'I think we'd be more comfortable back at the house, don't you?' she suggested hopefully. After she'd dressed, armoured herself against those steady, smoky, penetrating eyes.

'And have Blossom order us to make ourselves respectable and sit down to lunch like good children? I don't think so, do you?'

The apparent wry amusement was underpinned by a definite strand of steel. He looked and sounded like a man who would tell anyone who got in the way of what he wanted—and that included the redoubtable Blossom—to move! He'd obviously decided he was going to say whatever it was that had to be said right here, and if she didn't want an argument on her hands she'd have to do as she was told.

She'd give him five minutes. She wouldn't be able to stand being in his as-good-as-naked company for longer than that.

Not bothering to disguise her sigh of resignation as anything but just that, she sat, drawing her knees up to her chin and wrapping her arms around them. Hiding as much of herself as she could.

She would just have to try to pretend the sexual attraction wasn't there.

But it was going to be very, very difficult.

Fixing her eyes on the horizon, she asked, 'Well, what is it?'

She had no real reason to feel nervous, she reassured herself. Yesterday he'd got the message that she didn't want him to touch her, and last night he'd been kind. If you discounted the long years of enmity then superficially, at least, they were almost back to being buddies...

'Tell me what happened to our baby.'

The content of his question shocked her far more than that suddenly terse, unforgiving delivery. And then anger and loathing for his desertion of so long ago raged right through her. She twisted her head, scornful eyes raking his stony face.

'Why the interest now?' The pain of loss came flooding back. Her voice was harsh with it. She'd wanted that lost child so badly. 'Seven years ago, when it mattered, you were invisible!'

Her face set, she shot to her feet and swung round to stalk away, but a steel-fingered hand fastened around her ankle, shackling her.

'Let me go!'

'When I have an answer.'

Threat or promise, she was telling him nothing. He would have learned exactly what had happened from Vivienne, shrugged those impressive shoulders and got on with his life. She wasn't going to put herself through the agony of telling him about the worst few hours of her life, the following long period of grief and depression, just to satisfy his twisted curiosity.

She tried to jerk her foot away, but his grip simply tightened. His strength was formidable. It was a pity his character didn't match it!

'Have it your way.' Her mouth mutinous, she shuffled down in the sand, wondering if she could make a dash for it. The lean, tanned fingers slid away, releasing her. She decided she wouldn't do anything so undignified. He could make her sit here for ever, but he couldn't make her speak.

But her stubborn resolution was knocked sideways when he said bitterly, 'Let me put it another way. Why did you have an abortion? I was going to marry you, take care of you both.'

'I had *what*?' The words were shocked out of her. Her eyes flew to his harsh face, her brows knitting together as she tried to make sense of what he'd just said.

'You heard.' Impatience turned his eyes black. 'Just tell me why. I need to understand why you did it. When I do, I'll get out of your life and stay out.'

Threat or promise? she thought again, and wondered wildly why it felt more like a threat than the other. She felt suddenly nauseous and dizzy, and her fingers clutched the sand, but there was no substance, nothing to hold on to. Just as there would be nothing to hold on to if she never saw him again.

Which meant, she told herself wildly, that she was going mad!

She looked at him, at the tanned, oiled-satin skin that covered hard muscle and bone, the lean, lithe length of him, his masculinity only just covered by that wicked scrap of black fabric. She swallowed a moan and closed her eyes to block him out.

'You offered marriage out of duty. Because it was the right thing to do. When you heard what Harold said, on that awful day, you believed him. You didn't even bother to follow me to hear my side of it. You just let me go because I disgusted you,' she muttered.

Apart from one or two flashes of fighting spirit she'd been regressing ever since he'd turned up on the tiny island, and now she even sounded like her despised younger self—defensive and insecure.

She shivered, and he said heavily, 'I didn't follow you because—misguidedly, as it now appears—I was telling our dear departed stepfather not to blame you for his depravities. I didn't imagine you'd take off like a bat out of hell.' He gave a sharp, impatient sigh. 'Let's get you back to the house.' Suddenly he was on his feet, gathering up her belongings. 'You look as if you're about to faint. It's the heat. And you probably need food. We'll finish this conversation later.'

Georgia wished he wouldn't wait for her, but he did. And although he didn't touch her she was so achingly aware of him it was like being in purgatory. He kept shooting quick sideways glances in her direction, his dark brows drawn together, as if to satisfy himself she hadn't crumpled in a heap.

She had never fainted in her life; her pallor and light-headedness was down to shock, not a lack of food. As he stood aside for her to step on to the veranda she said firmly, 'I did not—'

'Not now,' he interrupted tersely. 'After lunch. And remember, I don't want to be fed a load of lies. I just want your reasons. Then I'll get out of your hair. We won't have to see each other again.'

It couldn't come quickly enough. He headed for

his room. When she'd come to his room that night seven years ago his head had been blown away by a mixture of patent flu remedies, alcohol, fever and sex. It was only later, when he'd learned of the consequences, that he'd realised how much he cared about her, how much he wanted that sweet, loving, sexy creature in his life. Wanted their child. Wanted to protect, love and cherish the two of them.

Now, his body still wanted her—more desperately than ever, he had to admit—but his intellect told him that she was about as sweet and loving as a queen wasp. A woman with attitude, as devious and self-seeking as they came. He remembered Vivienne, and grumpily decided it was bred in the bone.

He'd be off the island before the day was over. Out of reach of her aura of sinful temptation.

For the sake of his self-respect.

CHAPTER NINE

'You took your time!' Blossom pounced the moment Georgia entered the spacious, forest-facing dining room. 'Do I cook good food just to watch it spoil?' She exited with a crackle of her huge starched apron, and returned almost immediately with a heavily burdened tray. 'And that thing you're wearing needs a laundering. You got pretty things; why don't you wear them?'

Georgia took her place at the lunch table: elegantly laid for two and decorated with a bowl of delicate pink flowers which filled the air with fragrance.

'I changed into the first thing to come to hand,' she said airily, and told herself, Liar! You deliberately went for the cover of shirt and trousers. Then she wondered if she'd chosen to wear these same things yesterday, while she'd been waiting for Jason to arrive on the island, because she'd known deep inside her that the sex thing still fizzled between them and she'd been looking for protection. From herself. From him.

Blossom, muttering under her breath, set out a dish of spicy fried chicken, another of appetising mango, tomato and red onion salad, a platter of wafer-thin fried bread and a bowl of rice and peas, then stood back, her hands on her hips, waiting.

Georgia knew she was getting the 'fattening-up' treatment, and quailed. She wouldn't be able to get through a quarter of it, not the way she was feeling, her emotions in turmoil, her brain in a tangle over Jason's accusation. The sooner lunch was over and she could set him straight the better.

At least he could eat the lion's share of the food and deflect Blossom's wrath, she reflected as she helped herself to a little chicken and salad and spread it around her plate to make it look like a lot.

'Mr Jason, he just grabbed a sandwich,' Blossom grumbled, disabusing her. 'The generator's acting up, so he's fixing it. That Elijah's a no-good man—never around when he's needed!'

Left alone finally, Georgia ground her teeth with frustration. Jason had got the idea from somewhere that she'd got rid of their child, and from what he'd said he'd defended her against Harold's slur on her morality because he hadn't believed her capable of making sexual advances to her stepfather, not at that time.

But now he did. He probably thought she'd earned her inheritance by lying flat on her back!

The very idea made her feel ill. She gathered up most of the thin wafers of fried bread, walked on to the veranda through the open French windows and fed them to the birds. She felt the early-afternoon heat surround her, dewing her face with perspiration, sticking her clothes to her body.

The need to talk to Jason, put him straight, vindicate herself, was imperative. But heaven only knew how long it would take to fix the generator.

Blossom had a stand-by stove, which ran on bottled gas, and there were ample hurricane lamps, not to mention candles. But they needed the power supply for the huge refrigerator and deep-freeze. Jason wouldn't show until he'd finished the job. He took his responsibilities seriously.

As he had taken his responsibilities towards her and the child he had fathered seriously—enough to offer marriage, his care and protection.

Her stomach tightened with regret, with old memories of yearning, loving and needing. Simple, blind adoration. But that was the past, gone beyond recall, and this was the present. She was a different person, with different needs and aspirations.

She tossed the last of the bread to the chattering flock of birds and brushed the crumbs from her hands. There was only one constant, one threat that bound the past to the present.

Sex.

She walked back through the French windows and began to stack the lunch dishes on the tray Blossom had left on a mahogany side table. Sex. She could live without it. Had successfully done so for the last seven years. The price to be paid for emotional and physical involvement was way too high. Even if she hadn't had her own experience to draw on, she had her mother's.

She'd just put the record straight regarding that fictional termination, and then, as he'd said, he would leave. And she would let him go, and that would be the end of it. She would wipe the effect he, and only he, had on her from her mind and regain all her energy, drive and ambition—because that was what had made her the woman she was.

All she had to do was mentally let him go. Easy. Yet she wasn't so sure it would be quite so simple when she carried the tray through to Blossom and Jason walked through the outer door of the kitchen, wiping his strong, oil-streaked hands on a rag.

He was so gorgeous! That was the problem. Dark hair rumpled, a smudge of oil on one slashing cheekbone, his body emanating lean strength from the light covering of khaki drill shorts and loose black T-shirt.

Her heart juddered and the dishes clattered on the tray. The stark urgency of her physical need for him made everything inside her shake.

Blossom took the tray from her, tutting over the amount left uneaten.

After giving her a swift but encompassing look from under his brows, Jason tossed the rag in the waste bin and said, 'All fixed, Blossom. When Elijah gets back, ask him to be ready to ferry me over to San Antonio in time for this evening's airbus, would you?'

'You ain't leaving so soon, Mr Jason? Why, you only just got here!' Blossom wailed, dumping the tray on the sink with a clatter that boded ill for the delicate china. 'Whatever can you be thinking of?'

My sanity, Jason thought drily. My self-respect. I have to get out before I make a complete fool of myself and tell her I want her more than I've ever wanted any woman before or am likely to in the future.

To let himself be caught in the little witch's web again would be catastrophic. Love and trust was infinitely more important than lust, no matter how compelling.

He could no more trust her than he could sprout wings and fly.

He said, in passing, 'Needs must, I'm afraid, Blossom.' And to Georgia, his eyes cold, 'If I leave at four-thirty I'll have time to clean up, get changed and packed and see you at four to round off that conversation. So don't go missing.'

Or else, his tone implied, Georgia thought bleakly as she watched the door swing to behind him. Half an hour to tie up loose ends. Was that all he thought she rated? She gave a mental shrug. She wouldn't let it hurt. It wasn't worth it.

'And what conversation would that be, Miss Georgie?' Blossom wanted to know, her black eyes shrewd. 'You two been fightin'—is that why he's leavin' in such an almighty hurry?'

'Just some unfinished family business, that's all,' Georgia responded, as repressively as she knew how. 'And, no, we haven't been fighting.' Not the physical punch-on-the-nose variety, anyway.

'You two don't count as real family.' Blossom vigorously scraped the leavings into the waste bin. 'A stepfather in common, that's all you got. And just as well, in my opinion. My eyes near popped out of my head seeing you follow him out of the water wearin' just your skin!'

Turning on her heels, Georgia stalked out of the kitchen. Long before she gained the privacy of her room she felt her face go crimson with painfully deep embarrassment. Blossom had seen her, from here in the house or from the cliff edge, had thought they'd gone skinny-dipping together—and goodness only knew what else!

The humiliation wouldn't be nearly so great if they really had been enjoying—

No! She mustn't let herself think that way, conjuring up images of their naked bodies twined together in the silky water, of slow, exploring hands, of kisses that deepened until they were devouring each other, of a hunger that built until it exploded into a wild white heat that fused them together in the ultimate intimacy...

Grimly, she blanked out the erotic mental images, dragged off her crumpled clothes and stepped under the shower, adjusting the jet to cold. The heat seemed even more oppressive than usual now. Liberal dashes of cool cologne gave marginal relief. She brushed her wet hair and left it loose to dry.

He would have showered, too, by now. And packed. He hadn't appeared to have much in the way of luggage with him, so maybe he had never intended to stay for more than a couple of days. Maybe even less, if other things hadn't got in the way of what he had really come for. *Unfinished business.*

Things like the unreal, out-of-this-world happening down at the woodland pool, the discovery of the letter her mother had started to write. So what was he doing now? Passing time, leaving only the minimal amount of it to be spent with her, asking questions? Was he lying on his bed, naked, the paddle fans turning above his body, cooling him down?

She imagined his body as it had been this morning, tanned, lithe, sleek with water. Imagined it without the scrap of black fabric that had only just concealed his impressive manhood.

Just stop that! she told herself fiercely. Think of something else. Anything else.

What to wear? She padded to the built-in wardrobe and opened the sliding doors. No need to smother herself in all-concealing cotton, she thought rebelliously. She had nothing to hide that he hadn't seen before.

Not bothering with underwear, because the heat was sticky now, she plucked a silky scarlet sundress from its hanger and wriggled into it. Tiny straps supported a scooped-out bodice. She could see the outline of her nipples through the clingy fabric, the soft curve of her tummy before the skirt flared out slightly, ending midway down her thighs.

Provocative. She tossed her head, shaking her hair back from her face. She should worry! If he took one look at her and had a resurgence of the lust that had almost overcome the two of them down by the pool then there really wouldn't be a problem.

He had a boat to catch, a plane out to sanity and reason.

The minimum of make-up: a slick of moisturiser, a flick of mascara and a gloss of scarlet on her lips. All flags flying. They would never see each other again, and she wanted his last memory of her to be vibrant.

And that mattered to her. Probably much more than it should.

She spent the waiting time in the quietness of Vivienne's former room. She felt a deep empathy with her mother now, understood her, the way she'd acted. They'd both loved and been betrayed. The only difference between them was the outcome. Vivienne had had her child, and had bitterly resented the financial drain, the loss of freedom and the opportunity to have fun. Whereas she had lost the child she would have loved devotedly for the rest of her life.

She couldn't blame her mother for the way she'd acted. Different people handled disillusionment and pain in different ways.

She heard Blossom calling out for her and suddenly became aware of the rain, a heavy tropical downpour. She slipped out of the room, closing the door quietly behind her.

'So there you are. Mr Jason's looking for you. I put cold drinks in the sitting room.' Blossom's eyebrows rose when she saw the way the flirty scarlet dress clung, but she nodded her head in silent approval. 'Mr Jason tell me I won't be needed again today, so I'm off to my own place to finish up my ironing—that's if the rain don't drown me first!'

It was coming down in stair-rods; Georgia could hear it drumming on the roof. But it would stop as suddenly as it had started and everything would be back to normal—bright and sunny and serene. Just as she would be when Jason had taken himself out of her life again.

Which couldn't be soon enough. She was finding his presence increasingly hard to handle.

He was waiting for her. The room was dusky, the heavy cloud cover hiding the daylight. He turned from the long window, where he'd been watching the once placid waters of the cove turn to a heaving gun-metal-grey capped with foam as it crashed to the shore.

As his eyes swept from the top of her head to the tips of her bare toes and slowly back again she caught the dark glitter of his smoky eyes, the tightening of his hard jawline, and her heart punched her breastbone, her nipples tightening against the silky cradling fabric in unwitting response.

He couldn't hide the effect she had on him, she thought, with a wild and reprehensible stab of elation, and the way she'd chosen to dress was her only means of punishing him for making her body crave the magic of his.

And no chance of it rebounding on her because he would be leaving—she glanced up at the wall clock—in fifteen minutes!

She could play with fire and not get burnt!

'Before you say anything, Georgia, let's get one thing straight.' His voice sounded rusty, as if he had difficulty getting it to function. 'I'm not like your father. I don't run from responsibilities.' He was pouring gin into two tall glasses, topping it up with Blossom's tangy home-made lemonade. 'Earlier, you said you thought I'd believed what Harold said and dumped you because of it. I would have married you, provided for you and our child, regardless.'

He held out a glass to her and she stepped forward to take it, her fingers closing on the cool surface. Regardless of what? Of her coming on to Harold?

He didn't give her time to ask, said rawly, 'Was the fear that I might do what your father had done to your mother responsible for what you did? Was Vivienne's resentment of you, and the reason for it, the only thing you could see?'

Her throat tightened with anguish. Accusing her of rushing for an abortion was the cruellest thing he could throw at her. Worse, far worse, than his belief that she'd been having an affair with her own stepfather. That was simply too absurd to bother to refute.

He was watching her closely, waiting for her reaction, his hands pushed into the side pockets of his narrow-fitting fawn cotton trousers, his wide shoulders rigid beneath the black polo shirt he was wearing.

Let him wait. She swallowed half the contents of her glass, to ease the tension out of her throat, then put it carefully down on the glass-topped table that fronted one of the twin cretonne-upholstered sofas.

Lifting her chin, she told him coldly, 'For a supposedly intelligent man you get some lunatic ideas. I had a miscarriage and there are people who can verify that.' She looked pointedly at the wall clock. 'It's time you were on your way.'

It was enough. She couldn't say more. She couldn't talk about the lost child. Even after all these years it still hurt too much. She turned to walk out of the room but his voice stopped her. 'Say that again.'

Deliberately misinterpreting his brusque instruction, she reiterated tartly, 'It's time you were on your way. I know how desperate you are to leave. If you don't go now you'll miss the airbus.'

She willed him to go, to leave her, to set her free from the bonds of the past, the searing animal magnetism of the present. But he closed the space between them and asked her, 'Have you seen the state of the sea? I wouldn't ask anyone to put out in that. This isn't the normal tropical downpour, over almost as soon as it started. It's a full-blooded storm.'

The whine of the wind, the clatter of the rain— neither had registered since she'd entered the room. His presence took up too much space in her mind to allow room for anything else. And he was close enough now for her to see the texture of his skin, the sweep of the long lashes that veiled the glitter of his eyes.

He wasn't leaving! A rogue shaft of pleasure threaded through the welter of apprehension that made her breath catch in her throat, her heart beat faster. If she'd had the sense to note the state of the weather she would have known the seas were too wild to make the crossing to San Antonio anything other than downright dangerous. And she wouldn't have dressed this way!

Her wicked need to punish him might very well be her own undoing!

Desperately striving to keep any trace of panic out of her voice, she told him, 'What a bore for you. I'll leave you to contemplate your navel, then,' and swung away, stingingly aware of the flirtatious flick of her skirts, the way the soft fabric swung then settled back seductively against her thighs.

'Don't play games with me, Georgia!' His voice was soft, smoky-dark, but the hand that fastened on her shoulder, lean fingers biting the naked flesh, was steel-hard, inescapable. 'Teasing games could land you in more trouble than you can handle.' He swung her round to face him, their bodies almost touching, and the sexual tension made the air fizz as his eyes drifted from her parted lips, down the long, elegant line of her throat, down to the swelling curves of her breasts, the tell-tale hardening of her nipples that the soft clingy fabric did nothing to hide.

'Or is that what you want?' he asked thickly. 'Is that exactly what you're asking for?' The tips of his fingers were moving gently over her silky skin, both hands touching now, caressing her shoulders, easing the narrow straps out of the way.

Georgia felt herself catch fire, recognised the aching, heated quiver that began deep inside her, spreading upwards and outwards until her whole body came alive with the wanting. She sucked in her breath, caught the dark glitter of his eyes, and knew he was going to kiss her.

And knew she couldn't break free from the chains of desire that bound them together.

CHAPTER TEN

BUT he put her gently aside. She watched his eyes, saw the battle he fought with himself, saw him win. And put her knuckles against her mouth to stifle her cry of pain and rejection.

He was stronger than she. He could tear the chains asunder and set himself free.

Georgia would have walked out of the room if she'd been able to find the strength, but she barely had the power to stand. She sank slowly down on the end of the sofa, watching from beneath her long dark lashes as he reached for his glass and drained the contents.

Then she shuddered as he walked back towards her, her body reacting to him as it always had and always would. But he merely flicked on the table lamp at her side, so that she sat exposed in a pool of light while he leant against the long window in the dim, concealing shadows.

She wished she had his strength. Meeting him again had shown her that she wasn't anywhere near as tough as she'd thought she was. She hated the need that bound her to him, didn't want it. She didn't want the driven passion that pulsed between them, not without love.

She wanted his love, his trust. She wanted to be with him for the rest of her life.

The revelation hit her like a ton of bricks. She'd been hiding the truth from herself for such a long time.

And she knew the shock must be there on her face, because he said softly, 'I'm not going to throw things at you, or verbally rip you to pieces. I didn't follow you here to apportion blame, just to get at the truth.'

He had to grit his teeth until his jaw hurt to stop himself taking her in his arms and assuring her that he didn't bite. Or only very gently, and in all the right places.

He caught that thought and quashed it firmly. Thinking of kissing every inch of her delectable body was not a good idea. From the moment she'd walked into the room, sexy and sassy, standing her corner with her bare feet firmly planted on the ground, desire had eaten at him until his body could barely contain it.

Provocative witch. Clearly she wasn't wearing a thing under that seductive scrap she'd put on, with her long hair falling down her back, her mouth a pouting scarlet invitation.

Every damn thing about her was an invitation. An invitation he had to turn down because he knew what she was. Leaving the abortion aside—which now, apparently, she was set to deny—there was still the unsavoury business with Harold coming between them.

His mouth turned grim. There were too many unanswered questions surrounding that relationship. He didn't think he could hear the details without throwing up. So he wasn't going to ask.

Making sure that there was no hint of antagonism in his tone, to make her clam up and go on the defensive, he said, 'I was told on good authority that you'd had an abortion. So, OK, I know current thinking says a woman's body is her own, to do with as she wants, but it was my child too. I think I have the right to know what happened. And, more importantly, why it happened.'

A band of anguish tightened around Georgia's heart. Why was it possible to hold on to love for so long? The seeds had been sown ten years ago, had briefly blossomed, but they hadn't died, as she'd fooled herself into believing. Just grown stronger.

The bitterness of that past betrayal welling up and spilling over, she said, 'If it's so important to you, why did you take so long to ask questions? I left Lytham because I was frightened by what Harold had said. I might as well have stopped existing. You never once made contact. So why rake over it now?'

'I should have made contact,' he acknowledged darkly. He levered his long body away from the windowframe and began to pace the room, his hands bunched in his pockets, his shoulders tense. 'I might have prevented it, reassured you. I should have said to hell with my job; someone else can do it. But I didn't. I thought you were safe.'

'You're not making any sense,' she said, tight-lipped, keeping her jaw clamped to stop her teeth from rattling with tension. She didn't want to relive those dark days. Ever since she'd pulled herself up out of that pit of depression she'd done everything she could to forget. She never talked about it.

'No.' Suddenly the tension ebbed out of him. 'Perhaps I'm not.' He stopped pacing, sat on the opposite end of the sofa, angled towards her, his hands hanging loosely between his knees. 'I'll try to be coherent. That day—after I'd finished with Harold—I went to find you. Your car had gone. I hung around, waiting for you to come back. Then I phoned your friend's number. I'd guessed right. You were there. Sue's brother answered. He said you'd gone to bed; you were upset. I told him not to disturb you, asked him to tell you I'd phoned and would be in touch in a couple of days, to stay where you were and I'd come to pick you up and take you back to my apartment.

'I'd only intended to stay at Lytham long enough to tell you of the arrangements I'd made for us, and to break the news of our imminent marriage over dinner. I had to get back to London. I was briefing a barrister on behalf of a client in an important and complicated case of alleged fraud. I was working round the clock. Every evening I phoned Sue's number and got no reply. It didn't worry me too much at first; I knew you'd be OK with them. Finally, I phoned Lytham, thinking you might have gone back for some reason—to collect clothes—whatever.

'I told Vivienne I couldn't reach you at Sue's and she said she wasn't surprised. Apparently, later on the night you'd left Lytham, you'd phoned her, told her you were pregnant, asked where I was.'

'She said you'd already left, would have bought a ticket to the other side of the world—if you'd got any sense,' Georgia interjected miserably, painful memories bludgeoning her brain. 'She advised me to have an abortion and told me I would never be welcome at Lytham again. I'd always known she resented me, didn't like me. I hadn't known until then that she actually hated me.'

'Dear God!' Jason said thickly. 'And I wasn't there to help you.' He angled his head up, and there was deep regret in the eyes that held hers so steadily. 'Yes, she told me that she'd advised you to go for a termination, and that the problem was now sorted. Sue and her brother had picked you up from a private clinic that morning and taken you to their holiday home on the coast to recuperate.'

Georgia pushed her hair back off her face. Her hand was shaking. Jason reached out and covered it with his own. 'At least you now know how much she regretted her treatment of you. Had she lived, the two of you could have tried to build a good relationship.'

The comfort of his hand on hers was something she truly needed. Her fingers twined around his, clinging. Breathing shakily, she moistened her dry lips and told him what she had figured out a long time ago.

'Vivienne had to take Harold's side and believe implicitly in what he said. If she hadn't the marriage would have started to break down. It would have been the last thing she wanted at that time. She was in love with the lifestyle being married to a wealthy man gave her.'

His thumb was stroking the inside of her wrist now, and the inner yearning began to overwhelm her. Somehow she had to fight it, or she would shame herself by throwing herself at him again. And fighting him was easy when she dredged up the bitterness.

'So Vivienne told you what had happened about the baby and you heaved a sigh of relief and got on with your busy life.' Her voice tightened with remembered anguish, shook with it. 'A bunch of flowers and a card would have been a more civilised way of drawing a final line under the sorry episode. At least it would have shown you gave me a fleeting thought!'

She dragged her hand from his and he didn't try to recapture it. He went very still. Pain was etched in every line of his face. He said, 'I think we could both use another drink, don't you?' and pushed himself to his feet. His broad back was to her, shutting her out, as he refilled their glasses.

Georgia wiped the back of her hand across her brow. It was dark now, the storm abating, the air steamy with humidity. And what had been started, this long trawl through the past, had, of necessity, to be finished.

He turned and looked at her, a glass in each hand. 'That week—while I was back in London making arrangements for the wedding, all that stuff, putting my name on estate agents' mailing lists so that we could look for a suitable place to live—I learned a surprising thing about myself. I was totally, completely happy.'

He raised one brow sardonically, as if mocking that long-ago folly. 'I knew I wanted to be married. To you. You were sweet, loving—well, I'd always known that. What I hadn't realised was how much I'd grown to love you. I wanted you, and our child, and when I learned of the abortion I was too damned angry to trust myself to pick up a phone and speak to you, let alone go anywhere near you.'

He put the glasses on the table in front of her, looking down at her. She lowered her eyes, tightening her mouth. She couldn't bear it. He was all she had ever wanted and he had wanted her, too. There was no mistaking the sincerity in his voice. But it had all gone wrong.

Yet suddenly, gloriously, hope blossomed. The anger that had shattered everything for them had been misplaced. Vivienne hadn't told him everything. When he learned the truth, accepted it, then everything might come right for them.

She clutched the hope closely to her heart as he said, 'By the time I'd got myself into a calmer state of mind it was too late. You'd already left for America. You'd made no attempt to contact me. I knew then that our child and I had meant nothing to you. I set about wiping you out of my mind.' He raked his fingers through his hair. 'I'm telling you how it was. I'm not trying to make excuses, just giving you reasons.'

About to tell her that the mission to forget her had been pretty successful, until she'd got herself back in Harold's life, he changed his mind. They both had enough to contend with right now without opening up that particular can of worms.

He flopped down on the sofa facing the one she was using, energy draining out of him, sweat glistening along his hairline. It was so damned hot.

Georgia got to her feet and came to stand over him, and he closed his eyes because the seductive sway of her body, the sticky heat making the thin fabric cling to every inch of her, threatened to be a temptation too far.

'Jason.' She said his name softly, verbally reaching out to him with all the love in her heart, all the passion, all the need. 'I can't give you excuses, either. Just reasons. Everything happened so quickly. After I'd phoned Vivienne from Sue's I was frantic. You'd found me and Harold together and were too disgusted to want anything more to do with me, or so I thought. I went to my room and cried my eyes out for days, and Sue's brother never did give me that message. I guess he was in too much of a panic to remember.'

She took in a ragged breath as, for the first time, she talked about the loss of her baby, a loss she had never come to terms with. 'It was Sue who took charge when the pains started, called out their doctor—who took me to that clinic. Sue who stayed with me while I miscarried our child, who suggested they took me to the coast to recuperate and then to New York—very much earlier than we'd originally intended.'

She saw his eyes bat open, the sharp glitter in the smoky grey depths, heard the inward tug of breath into his lungs and knew that she had reached him, that at last he had listened to her, believed her. 'I went because I hadn't heard from you, and because I no longer cared what happened to me,' she told him quietly. 'I wanted to contact you but wouldn't let myself. I was eighteen years old, totally insecure, deeply unhappy—because I'd lost what I most wanted in the world, both you and our child, and I couldn't bear to hear you tell me to get lost.'

'A miscarriage?' He was struggling to come to terms with the sudden reversal of all his opinions. 'Vivienne told me you'd—'

'No,' she interrupted gently, resisting the impulse to reach out physically, touch the side of his face with her hand. 'Think about it. From what you said, she told you the problem was "sorted". Sue had given her the news, and, yes, Vivienne had advised an abortion, but I never for one moment considered that as an option.'

She held her breath. Waiting. Deep in her bones she knew that everything hinged on whether he really believed her or not. True, there were medical records that could be checked, and Sue and her family would be only too happy to verify her story. But she needed him to believe her. Implicitly.

Briefly, he struggled with shock. The anger that had consumed every rational instinct in its wild flames, turning to the cold ashes of hatred, had been for nothing. He dragged in a harsh breath. Appalled.

'Georgia.' Raw emotion roughened his voice as he reached out, put his hands on her hips and pulled her towards him, resting his head against the soft curve of her tummy. 'I should have been there for you and I wasn't. I won't forgive myself for that.'

'Don't!' she whispered brokenly. Talking about the trauma to him, the father of her lost child, had helped, taken away the pain. Threading her fingers through his soft dark hair, holding him closer, her hips swaying, moving against the side of his face, feeling the hard jut of his jaw, his slashing cheekbone press into her body, swaying because she simply couldn't help it, because it was as natural, as right, as drawing breath, she said, 'It's over. It's the past. We both let our emotions blind us to reality. Please— please, let's start over.'

The musky scent of female arousal, the seductive, enticing, inviting movements of her fantastic body, the softness of her and the heat of her beneath the fine barrier of silk sent every rational and reasonable thought straight out of his head.

There was only need, the driving, burning savage need building inside him, until he could contain it no longer. Didn't try.

Remorse, regret, and the urgency of desire were forces too powerful for him to fight. He turned his head into the softness of her, opened his mouth against the slippery scarlet silk and kissed her, and felt her gyrate for him. With a savage groan he slid his hands down the curve of her hips, moving them under her short, flirtatious skirt, cupped the flesh he'd known would be naked, brought his hands round and slipped to his knees. Lost and not regretting it. No room in his head for regrets. No room for anything but sweet Georgia and what she did to him.

With a tortured moan he pushed her skirt up to her waist, exulting in his dominion over her as she compliantly, instinctively, moved her small bare feet apart, her pelvis jutting forward, eager for him.

He shuddered as his mouth found the soft hair guarding her womanhood, felt the tips of her fingers convulse against his skull, and knew that this was what he'd wanted, dreamed of, ached for, ever since she'd come back into his life.

She was eager, she was sweet, she was moist, musky heaven. He suckled her womanhood and she was nectar, and she was his. He felt her body turn to boneless jelly beneath his supporting hands, heard her small, thick cries of pleasure and stood, sweeping her into his arms in one driven movement, and laid her down on the sofa, catching his breath as she looked at him with desire-drenched eyes, fumbling blindly for his zip.

Her fingers were shaking. He covered them with his own, helping her, and when her arms lifted to wind around his neck he went down to her, and into her, into the slick, welcoming heat of her, and heard her gasp of exultation, of wonder, heard it mingle with his own and felt his muscles grow tense with the effort of holding back, slowing down, making it as good for her as he knew it would be for him.

But her body writhed beneath him, her movements driven and wild, and his precarious control went, just went, and all that was left was the savage urge to fulfilment, and the long, shuddering cries of release that came together in the steamy air.

CHAPTER ELEVEN

GEORGIA stretched her deliciously sated body. Not easy on the sofa, her limbs tangled bonelessly with Jason's, their bodies so close they could have been one. But the difficulty was sweeter than honey, more exciting than the most fiendish white-knuckle ride invented.

They must have slept for hours. 'I'm hungry,' she told him soporifically, then gasped as she felt his body's immediate and deeply satisfying response to her languorous movement. 'Ravenous,' she added throatily.

He groaned thickly as his mouth sought the soft hollow at the base of her throat, savouring the honeyed warmth of her skin with tiny kisses that traced the valley between her breasts. 'Me, too.'

Half drowsing in the aftermath of passion's storm, drenched in the joy of loving him, the miracle of knowing that the barren years were behind them and that the future beckoned, promising joy, fecund with a love no longer blighted by past misconceptions, she'd felt ravenous for food.

But not now. Oh, no, not now. His love was all the sustenance she needed. She ran her fingers over his back, the hard muscle and bone beneath the satin skin, and this time their loving was slow, exquisitely, tormentingly slow, and afterwards, still joined together in the closest intimacy there is, Jason hoisted himself up on one elbow and gently pushed the damp hair away from her face, his mouth sensual, soft, his veiled eyes holding the hazed golden jewels of hers.

'Are you OK?' Concern, tenderness laced his voice, and she ran the tips of her fingers down his ribcage, angling forwards to feather down over the taut muscles of his stomach to where their bodies joined.

'What do you think?' Her smile was wicked. Unused muscles might feel sore, but that was a tiny price to pay for such happiness, such glorious peace. The lost years meant nothing now they had found each other again.

He didn't answer her smile. 'I meant about what happened, the baby. You must have felt betrayed. I know I did at that time—wrongly so, as it happens. It must have been so much worse for you.' He placed a gentle kiss on the bridge of her nose. 'I can't tell you how much I admire your courage in finding the strength to put it all behind you, to go on. You must have put every scrap of your energy into getting where you are with the agency, becoming the woman you are today.'

'I coped.' She dismissed the years of total, grinding dedication to her work. They were meaningless. Loving him was the only thing of value. And there was no difference between the woman she was today and the eighteen-year-old who had conceived his child. She was still besotted, adoring. Probably more so. Definitely more so.

'I'm fine now, truly. Everything's sorted out and we know that neither of us was to blame for what happened.' She trailed her fingers over the dark sockets of his eyelids, the sharp angle of his cheekbones, easing the shadows away, and sensed the relief her words and loving gesture had brought him. She saw his mouth soften into a smile as he took her hand and kissed the backs of her fingers.

'I think we should get more comfortable. I gave up sleeping on sofas after my student days.'

Scooping her and their abandoned clothes into his arms he carried her to her bedroom, slid her slowly down the length of his body, dropped their clothes on the floor and opened the shutters to the golden promise of another brilliant dawn.

'A shower, then I'll fix our breakfast.' His eyes gleamed at her. 'I feel like spoiling you, so don't go all feminist on me and ruin my fun!'

She had no intention of doing anything of the sort, and wound her arms around his neck as he carried her through to the *en suite* bathroom and under the shower where he lovingly soaped every inch of her body as the warm water cascaded over them.

'If this is being spoiled, I'm fully in favour,' she told him with a sybaritic sigh of sheer pleasure as he at last patted her dry with a fluffy towel, then pooled perfumed body oil into the palm of his hand.

'This is only the beginning, I promise you. All you have to do is stand there and enjoy.'

'Enjoy' didn't come anywhere near describing the exquisite torment as he massaged oil into every pore of her skin, each sensual stroke of his hands a seduction in itself, and by the time he was hunkering down, circling her ankles and slender calf muscles with slow, spiralling movements, she was almost fainting with the intensity of pleasure.

'Jason—please—' She gripped his wide shoulders to steady herself, her whole body quivering, heat flaming through her, scorching every cell until she thought she would explode in white-hot flames if he didn't assuage the wild longing inside her.

'Patience.' His dark, sexy voice was laced with humour as he stood upright and twisted a towel around his lean waist. 'Breakfast first. Hop into bed and I'll bring it to you. You'll need to keep your strength up, considering what I've got in mind for you over the next few days.' His voice suddenly sobered, his brows lowering over darkening eyes as he promised, 'I'm going to make love to you until your head's reeling, until all the bad things are wiped out and our lovemaking is the only thing you remember.'

Georgia dismissed his sudden and unexpected return to gravity. Her head was reeling already. She watched him walk out of the room, devouring the way the tanned skin lay tight and inviting over wide rangy shoulders, the muscles of his back tapering to the towel-covered lean hips, the long, perfectly proportioned, hair-roughened legs.

She gazed at the door for minutes after he'd closed it behind him, her eyes glittering with sudden tears.

She didn't know what she had done to deserve such a wealth of happiness.

Then she blinked and walked to the bed, glorying in her perfumed nakedness. She had been made for this, for this one man, had known it since the first time she'd seen him. She hadn't been celibate for seven years because, as she'd told herself so often, she didn't trust emotional involvement, but because there was only one man for her.

And the next few days, the ones he had talked about, would only be a prelude to the rest of their lives. She wouldn't have to remember the passion of his lovemaking because that, too, would be with them always.

She flopped on the top of the coverlet and piled pillows up behind her. There were plenty for him, too, but when he carried a tray through he sat at the foot of the bed, then swung his long legs up, lacing them with hers, the tray balanced between them.

'Now I can watch you eat,' he told her, smoky eyes glinting. 'I intend to cram everything possible into this escape from reality.'

Fleetingly, she thought to remind him that this, their rediscovery of each other, their loving, was as real as it got, but he leaned forward and popped a morsel of sweet, juicy pineapple between her parted lips.

He'd sliced all the fruits he could lay his hands on—mangos, strawberries, and the highly perfumed and slightly tart soursops balancing sweet banana slices and luscious grapes.

Georgia said, 'I'm starving, but if we eat all this and Blossom comes in to prepare our breakfast—'

'She won't.' He selected a plump, ripe strawberry and rubbed it over her lips until she took it between her teeth. 'I put a note on the kitchen table telling her we'd eaten and that apart from wanting her to put together a picnic lunch we'd be looking after ourselves. So quit worrying.' He grinned at her suddenly. 'You may be the boss lady back at the agency, but I'm in charge of your well-being and pleasure— with particular emphasis on the pleasure aspect—for the next few days.'

There it was again, the mention of a few days. Maybe he was too busy to stay longer. In that case she'd cut her own holiday short and return to England when he did. She couldn't bear to be here without him. Couldn't bear to be without him, full-stop.

'We could borrow Elijah's boat and visit the other side of the island—as I recall, it's littered with isolated, sheltered cays,' he suggested when they'd eaten their fill of the delicious fruit. 'Unless you fancy trudging up the spurs and hacking a way through the forest?' He buttered a slice of cornbread and handed it to her. 'The cove on the doorstep here isn't nearly secluded enough for what I have in mind.'

She knew exactly what he had in mind. Her throat tightened and her heart began a wild tattoo. Around him she was in a permanent state of arousal.

The bread dropped from her suddenly nerveless

fingers, back on to the plate, and Jason leant over to put the tray down on the floor, then looked deep into her wide, expressive eyes.

'I know,' he said softly. 'I know.' And he lifted the small foot that was tucked against his hip bone and began to suckle her toes.

'I could get used to island life!' Georgia murmured pleasurably as she wriggled her bottom into the soft cushions of the comfy cane chair. She eyed Jason over the silver coffee pot and delicate china cups the waiter was placing exactly so on the tabletop.

Jason looked particularly edible this morning. Over the past five days his tan had deepened spectacularly, and his dark hair needed the attentions of the top-flight barber he obviously used. But she liked it that way. With the fine cotton black collarless shirt opened down to his waist, where it tucked into narrow-fitting white trousers, it gave him a buccaneering look that completely turned her on.

Yet everything about him turned her on, she admitted, grinning at him as the waiter moved away. She had never, in the whole of her life, been happier. Never felt so feminine, so sexy, so utterly ravished!

'There's no reason why you shouldn't. You already own one of them.' He returned her smile, but his was guarded. He poured coffee for them both, concentrating on that, and Georgia watched him from under her lashes and turned his words over in her mind very carefully.

She had wondered. Jason hadn't proposed, and he

hadn't said he loved her. But every touch, every look told her that he did. It was unthinkable that they wouldn't spend the rest of their lives together, but the idea of living in this paradise with Jason was almost too wonderful and perfect to comprehend.

Thanks to Harold's legacy neither of them need work for a living ever again. But Jason possessed a fierce ingrained pride that would baulk at the mere thought of living off her money. Not for the first time she wished Harold had divided his assets equally between his stepchildren.

But they could certainly spend every holiday on Blue Rock... She allowed her thoughts to drift, soaking up the atmosphere of San Antonio's most exclusive hotel. They were sitting outside on the pillared open piazza, amongst tubs of perfumed flowering shrubs, with a glorious view over the hotel's manicured lawns. The spreading branches of enormous cotton trees made a leafy frame for the natural harbour below, where the yachts of the seriously wealthy were moored.

When Jason had suggested visiting San Antonio this morning because he needed to make a couple of phone calls, and he couldn't do that from Blue Rock, she had immediately agreed, and now she remembered him saying, 'Elijah will be glad to see the back of me. He must be desperate to have the use of his boat. Going fishing is his only way of getting away from Blossom's sharp tongue!'

'We could hire a boat,' she told him now, stirring her coffee, enjoying the tiny sound of the silver spoon clicking against fine china. The smallest, most surprising things gave her pleasure since she and Jason had come together again. 'It would give Elijah his freedom back. What do you think?'

It seemed the fairest thing to do. Stuck at base, poor Elijah would be getting restless, with Blossom constantly on his case, chivvying him to do this, that and the other chore around the place when he obviously preferred to shift himself 'when the spirit moved him'.

And they would still have the means of getting to the farthest side of the island, anchoring off one of the uninhabited cays that lay in the shelter of the reefs, as they had been doing for the past five days. Taking one of Blossom's lavish picnics, swimming, drowsing on the hot white sands, making love...

Jason took his time responding. Georgia leant back in her chair and relaxed. They, too, seemed to be living on island time, the pace slow and dreamy. Magical. As divorced from the reality of everyday life as the distant millionaires' mansions that could be glimpsed in wide clearings carved into the forest that clothed the high hills of the interior.

With a sigh of pleasure, she leaned forward and refilled their coffee cups, her smile faltering when she saw the lines of tension suddenly carve into his darkly handsome face, making him look austere— lines that had been absent recently.

He caught the slight query in her long-lashed golden eyes and his heart hurt.

She'd twisted her hair up on top of her head this

morning, and feathery tendrils had escaped to frame her lovely, sun-kissed face. The chocolate-coloured top she was wearing left her golden arms and most of her slender shoulders naked, lovingly cradled her firm breasts and then came to a full-stop, leaving several inches of midriff bare above the waistband of her tiny white shorts.

Tantalising, sexy, incredibly desirable. The hard edges of the Georgia who had come back into his life such a short time ago had been rubbed away now. Their time together, after the misconceptions of the abortion that never was had been cleared away, had done that for her. They had both needed an escape from reality, needed their fantasy time, their healing time.

But now it was time to end it, to draw a line under this period of adjustment and move on.

Long after she'd fallen asleep in his arms last night he'd lain awake, thinking it over. Nothing lasted for ever, not even paradise. He'd known it would be difficult to say goodbye, but hadn't realised just how difficult until he'd seen the query in her eyes.

Now he had to answer it.

'It's a possibility,' he responded to her suggestion. 'But unless you're confident you can handle a boat, I wouldn't advise it.' Something twisted fiercely in his gut at the thought of walking out of her life. He ignored it because he had to, and explained gently, 'I won't be with you. There's an air taxi out later this afternoon, and I'm hoping to arrange a connecting flight from St Vincent. Failing that, I'll book into a hotel in Kingstown and wait on standby.'

For long, silent moments she didn't understand what he was saying, and then she did. Their island idyll was over, and the drag of disappointment went right down to her toes.

She recovered immediately. For pity's sake, they didn't need azure seas and sparkling sunshine to be happy! Wherever he went, she needed to be. Besides, he had a high-profile job to get back to, and he took his responsibilities seriously.

'Of course.' She flashed him a commiserating smile. 'You'll need to get back to work; I understand that. No problem. I'll come with you.'

She drained the last of her coffee, making rapid mental plans. Do his business here, a forty-minute boat trip back to Blue Rock, pack, tell Blossom and Elijah goodbye. Assure them she had no intention of selling up, that their home, their livelihood was safe. And forty minutes back again to catch the late-afternoon air taxi—Elijah would ferry them. No problem.

Her soft, kissable mouth was set in the determined line he had come to know so well, and her golden eyes were glittering with the excitement of moving on. But it wouldn't work, couldn't work.

He would never want another woman the way he wanted her, but that was his problem, and he wasn't going to compound it by allowing the relationship to go any deeper. Any deeper and he'd be bound to her for ever. And he couldn't do that with the spectre of Harold in the background.

Harold, whether he'd been telling the truth or not about who had been coming on to who, had caused the complete breakdown of Georgia's already troubled relationship with her mother. Yet he'd flown out to New York, after Vivienne's funeral, and everything had been hunky-dory. Harold had kept all her letters—which Jason hadn't been able to bring himself to read—and lunched with her at monthly intervals after her permanent return to England.

Jason had tried to dismiss it as quasi-fatherly interest, but he hadn't succeeded. One look at the spectacularly gorgeous new Georgia, coupled with the knowledge of what his stepfather had been like—and knowing what he'd known about the legacy—had turned ugly suspicions into near certainties.

And she'd clinched the whole thing herself. He recalled the taunt he'd flung at her, not believing she'd refused Harold's advances—'Because as sure as God made little green apples he wouldn't have left his entire fortune to you if you had.' He'd hated himself for the jibe even as the words had left his mouth. But she'd simply given him that cool, clever look of hers and calmly congratulated him on how astute he'd become.

That certainly hadn't been the hot denial he knew he'd been secretly hoping for. It had made him hate her for what she'd become.

Yet, looking at her now, he could only want her, couldn't hate her. The violent emotion had been stopped in its tracks the moment he'd learned the truth about what had happened to their unborn child.

His heart had bled for her, for what she must have gone through, and the rest, as they say, was history.

But he couldn't tell her why there was no future for them. Not if he wanted to keep his sanity. He couldn't spell his reasons out; he couldn't humiliate her that much.

She was verbalising her plans for a swift getaway, and he cut across the breathless words, explaining gently, 'Georgia—I'm a senior partner now; I don't have to get back if I don't want to. In my position, it's easy to delegate. But it's time I went.' High time, if he didn't want to become totally, irretrievably addicted. 'And I think it's best if you stay on, finish your holiday.'

He watched her eyes widen, some of the animation leave her face, and had to force himself not to retract those words, take her in his arms and tell her he wanted her with him always. Needed her.

He had to make himself say, 'We both needed these last few days. Needed to close the circle, give each other back the peace that the last seven years of misunderstanding deprived us of.'

And for him that was the truth. The whole truth. He had been able to put what she had become out of his mind, concentrate solely and completely on his instinctive need to make her happy and, yes, to make love to her, possess her utterly and wholly.

'And now it's time to draw a line under the past, close the book and go our separate ways.' The words stuck in his throat, he had to push them out, and in doing so probably sounded harsher, colder, than he'd had any intention of doing.

He regretted that, hated the look of shock in her eyes, the way her colour fell away beneath her golden tan, hated himself for being the cause of it. He had to remind himself that Georgia could look after herself now; she didn't need him.

She was more than financially secure, she was an extremely wealthy woman, and if she needed physical consolation—and it was his guess she would, and soon, because she was one hell of a sexy lady—then she had her live-in lover to fall back on.

He had actually forgotten the guy's existence, but reminding himself of it had stopped him doing what he'd been tempted to do—taking her hands, telling her he'd always be there for her, thus opening the way for future meetings, prolonging the agony.

'If that's what you really want.' It had taken a few moments, but she was now back in control. Drawing on the harsh lessons she'd learned over the past seven years, she pushed the racking pain, the overwhelming feeling of loss and emptiness, right to the back of her mind. 'Then it's absolutely fine by me.'

She plucked her sunglasses from the top of the table and put them back on, hiding her eyes, unwilling to have him know how shattered she was inside, how near she had come to breaking apart, going down on her knees and begging him not to cut her out of his life. 'Shouldn't you make those phone calls? You don't want to cut it too fine.' She got to her feet, willing her legs to hold her upright. 'I'll wait for you at the harbour.'

'Georgia—' He had got to his feet, towering over her. Again she had to summon all her inner strength to fight the humiliating desire to burst into tears, cling to him, beg him not to leave her, not ever, to tell him how much she loved him. In a turmoil of emotion she heard him say, his voice soft, 'Don't think I won't remember these last few days—'

'Oh—please!' She had to stop him. She just had to! If he tried to be kind then she would go to pieces; no amount of will-power could stop that happening. 'Spare us both. It was fun while it lasted. Let's just take that as read.' And she turned her back and walked away, and felt the scalding heat of tears on her face.

CHAPTER TWELVE

FOR once traffic on the motorway was relatively light, and although the winter morning was overcast it was at least dry. Georgia glanced in her mirrors, indicated, pulled over into the fast lane and put her booted foot down and listened to the engine sing. Her hands were feather-light on the steering wheel, and she felt herself begin to relax for the first time since her happiness had been so cruelly shattered on San Antonio.

She'd left Blue Rock twenty-four hours after Jason, and had spent the two days she'd been back in England adjusting to the change in temperature, readjusting to the prospect of a loveless future and trying to decide what to do with the rest of her life.

One thing was certain: she wouldn't be looking back.

So work would fill her future, of course; there wasn't anything else. No plans now for marriage and children. That cosy scenario was right out of the frame. And she only had herself to blame for the misery and heartache. She'd forgotten all she'd learned and let her emotions rule her head.

She'd been seriously considering giving the bulk of her inheritance away to charity, because she had no real use for it; she could support herself. She needed her work, needed it to fill her mind. She'd just keep enough back to buy herself a small home in the country, within reasonable travelling distance of the agency, because since her return from the Caribbean Ben had made her flat untenable, forever hovering, hanging around, leaving when she told him to but always, always coming back.

Yes, she had been planning to spend the day trawling round the local estate agents when the phone call had come from Harold's solicitor.

She throttled back, brake-lights flashing, when she saw the advance warning signs for roadworks ahead, automatically glancing in her rearview mirror, noting the silver Jaguar.

Keeping her speed down, she filtered into the contraflow system. She hadn't meant to be returning to Lytham Court so soon, if ever. But Harold's solicitor had said, making it sound like a mystery, 'A letter has turned up, addressed to you, with the instruction that you read it only in the event of your stepfather's death. Mrs Moody, quite rightly, handed it to me. Now...' She had heard the rustle of papers and wondered what on earth Harold had wanted to say to her that couldn't have been said while he was still alive, and then the solicitor had gone on, 'I've also got papers here that need your signature—pertaining to the provisions you wish to make for Mrs Moody and Albert Baines out of your late stepfather's estate. As I would like them both to be present, I suggest I meet you all at Lytham—three this afternoon would suit me, if you can make it. Otherwise, perhaps you could suggest some other day.'

She'd told him that today would be fine. Might as well get it over with. She wasn't due back at work until the beginning of next week. House-hunting would have to wait until tomorrow.

The sign for rejoining the main carriageway was in front of her; the silver Jaguar was still hugging her tail. Nice car, she thought idly, with elegant, classic lines.

Past the last of the cones, the traffic sped up, and the Jaguar kept close company; she would almost miss it when she left the motorway. But it was right behind her as she cut back her speed on the exit road, and she wondered if she could lose him on the trunk road ahead.

Of course she could! The prospect filled her with the first feeling of being alive she'd experienced since Jason had effectively told her, Wham-bam, thank you, ma'am, and walked right out of her life.

As she depressed the accelerator she felt the eager, thrusting response of the powerful engine in every cell of her body, and this was the type of road she enjoyed—plenty of straights spiced with fast, open curves, and just enough traffic to challenge her driving skills.

She overtook an articulated lorry and slipped back on to her side of the road in a single, neat manoeuvre. A brief glance in her mirror told her that her silver shadow was still with her, and its headlights flared—in challenge or in warning?

The needle hovered around ninety miles per hour. She reined in the engine until it dropped to a sober eighty. Let him pass, if he wanted to. The driver was either the macho type, who couldn't bear to see a woman in front of him, or, horror of horrors, a policeman in an unmarked police car!

He didn't pass, just stayed in her slipstream. She was beginning to feel distinctly annoyed, the exhilaration of driving to the best of her considerable ability ebbing away because she couldn't shake him off her tail.

They were approaching a largish village, and she slowed, sticking strictly to the speed limit, ignoring the silver Jaguar behind. Once past the traffic lights, a couple of miles on, she would be turning off into a tangle of country lanes, heading for Lytham. It would be too much of a coincidence if he was also heading that way.

She braked gently at some traffic lights, and although she'd told herself to ignore the irritating driver behind curiosity got the better of her, and she lifted her eyes to her rear-view mirror and took a long, hard look.

Jason! She felt herself go white, every ounce of strength draining from her body until her limbs were shaking.

As far as she was concerned, he was nothing but bad news.

His first betrayal she could now understand and forgive, because it had been the result of a massive misconception. The second she could understand—

he'd wanted sex and she'd been willing—but she would never forgive. The hurt had been too much.

The lights changed, and, half stupefied, she eventually found the right gear and eased across the junction.

He was still following her, and that she would not tolerate. Unless, the thought flickered, he too had been summoned to Lytham. But why should he have been?

She would find out soon enough. She indicated well ahead of the turn-off to the narrow minor roads, and, yes, he was turning, too.

Tense, her jaw clamped tightly, she drove slowly, looking for the right place, then found it, braking, pulling the car into a passing place that had been carved out of the verge.

She pressed the switch that let down the window at her side and cold air filled the car. She waited, her mouth grim, her eyes shadowed with the pain she could do nothing about.

The silver car swerved to a halt in front of her, and in moments he was striding back to her, long legs encased in mole-grey cords, wide shoulders rigid beneath a soft leather jacket, his face furious.

Almost as if she had known what he would do, she glued herself to the leather bucket seat and waited for the onslaught as he dragged open the door and bit out, 'You could have killed yourself!'

She didn't want to see him, to see his hauntingly handsome face. She didn't want to talk to him either, but she had to because she wasn't taking that!

She turned her face to his, her expression stony, and said, very precisely, her anger precariously contained, 'No. I drive a fast car well. I don't take risks. I know what I'm doing. If there was any danger it was because you were tail-gating.'

He ignored her words completely. 'Get out!' And before she could react he leant over her, taking the keys from the ignition, his hands clamping on her shoulders as she sat immobilised by an anger so intense she thought she might explode with it.

Impatiently, he slid his hands under her arms and hauled her out, and only when her booted feet met the grass of the verge did she find her tongue. She lashed him with it. 'If you don't get your hands off me and give me my keys I'll have you prosecuted for assault. The police take road rage very seriously.'

'Shut up!' he snapped through his teeth, and wound an arm around her narrow waist, lifting her off her feet and carrying her, kicking and wriggling. He pushed her into the back seat of his car and slid in beside her.

Slithering round, she felt all the emotion she'd suppressed since he'd ended their brief island affair boil over as she slapped his face. Through a red mist of rage she saw his mouth tuck in at the corners, heard him do what she'd least expected—apologise.

'I'm sorry. This wasn't meant to happen.' He ran the fingers of one hand through his hair, rumpling it, and said, his voice rough, 'When she knew her relationship with Harold was over your mother came back to Lytham and collected her car—with tragic results. I thought you—'

Before he could offer the final insult to her character she stopped him with an oath worthy of a building site worker in a temper, then offered scathingly, 'I am *not* my mother. I don't go to pieces behind the wheel of my car—or anywhere else, for that matter—just because a man turns out to be a bastard. I *expect* a man to be a bastard!' She held out a hand. 'Now give me my keys.'

Jason's heart lurched as he looked into the burnished, glittering gold of the eyes that dominated the frozen features of her gorgeous face.

All the hard edges were back in place; she'd rebuilt that fortress. She was sexy, tough, had attitude. And he loved her. Despite her muddy relationship with Harold. He couldn't blame her for that, not if he viewed the subject rationally, put his possessiveness where she was concerned aside.

She'd felt betrayed, rejected by her lover and her parent, barred from her home. Ignored. Harold had been the only one who had had anything to do with her, shown her any affection.

It didn't matter that she'd turned to the only one of them who hadn't treated her like a pariah. He could understand it, shut it away in the past where it belonged, along with all the other emotional baggage—sleepless nights since he'd left her on the island had shown him that. He prayed to God it wasn't too late.

'No.' He denied her demand for the keys. 'I want to talk to you.'

'I can't think why.' She didn't avoid his eyes, didn't so much as blink. She would show him she could outface him. 'You already thanked me for giving you a few days of good sex.' She made a leisurely production of looking at her wristwatch. Loads of time, but he didn't know that. 'I've an appointment with Harold's solicitor at Lytham. I don't intend to keep him waiting.'

'Georgia—just shut up.' His voice had dropped, was soft as honey now, and the expression in his eyes reminded her of the way he had looked at her when everything had been so briefly wonderful. She couldn't bear it. She lowered her eyes, swiftly veiling her own expression as she brushed an imaginary fleck from the knee of the tailored mulberry-coloured trousers she was wearing.

'I love you,' he said, and there was a strange catch in his voice. 'But that's nothing new. The only problem is, I can't imagine life without you. And I'm a big enough fool to have overlooked that glaringly obvious fact.' He took one of her hands in both of his and added carefully, as if he were mentally walking on eggshells, 'Could a bright lady like you possibly marry a fool?'

Paralysed by the unexpected, Georgia let her hand stay in his, feeling his thumb slide back and forth over her clenched knuckles. She lifted her eyes, not looking at him, not daring to—hardly daring to breathe even—and fixed them on the winter-bare trees and fields she could see through the windscreen.

Was this a cruel trick? Or was she dreaming, putting words into his mouth that he hadn't said? Or had his final betrayal of her love for him pushed her right over the edge? Was she going crazy?

'If you say no, I'll understand. I'll hate it, but will understand. I had to find you and ask. I was cursing myself for being such an idiot, cutting myself off from the only woman I've ever loved, long before the plane to Heathrow touched down. I've been sleepless at night, thinking of you, wanting you. Desperate. So afraid I'd lost you again through my own stupidity.' Briefly the pressure of his fingers tightened, and then relaxed. 'I drove up to Birmingham to tell you all this, saw your car leave the street as I turned into it, and came after you.'

His heart thumped, constricting his breathing. If she didn't respond soon he'd take her in his arms and kiss her until she was forced to, kiss her until the frozen features glowed with the vibrancy that was so much a part of her. He wouldn't be able to stop himself.

Following her car, he'd admired the way she drove, entranced by the flirty, sexy package of sports car and driver. Then he'd remembered Vivienne's fate, and couldn't recall ever having been so terrified.

'Marry me, Georgia,' he said with thick urgency.

The landscape in her vision blurred and tilted because her brain was going haywire. If he'd asked her a few days ago, instead of saying, Thanks, it was nice knowing you, and catching the first flight out of her life, she'd have accepted like a shot and known she was in heaven.

But that was then. This was now, and she'd spent much time and energy transforming herself back into the hard-nosed tough career woman she'd been before. The woman who didn't need anyone. The woman who didn't get hurt because she never let anyone close enough.

'Georgia. Tell me you don't love me and you get more than your keys; you get your life back. But if you *do* love me, and after our time together on the island I believe you do, then I get the rest of your life to cherish and hold dearer than my own. And you get mine, to do with as you will.' One of his hands cupped the delicate line of her jaw, tilted her head. 'Look at me.'

She met his smoky, smouldering eyes and lost herself. Lost the dedicated career lady and found the woman who'd been born to love this one man.

Her mouth softened, trembled. Tears rushed to her eyes and clogged her throat, and she couldn't have spoken if her life had depended on it.

His hand slid to the back of her head as he shifted closer, kissing away the crystal drops, working down to her mouth and taking that, tasting her tears, her lips, deepening the kiss to accommodate her electrifying wild response.

'I take it that's a yes?' he murmured huskily as she broke away at last, pulling breath into her starved lungs, her soft lips tingling.

She nodded, her eyes sparkling with tears of almost unbearable happiness. 'Yes,' she whispered unsteadily. 'If you're sure? I couldn't bear it if—if you just went away again—'

'Sweetheart...' He groaned, pulling her close, holding her against his heart. 'I'll never do anything to hurt you again, and that's a promise.' He felt her small hands flutter beneath his jacket, felt the warmth of her through his light sweater, and felt his flesh shake with the power of his need for her, loving her more than he'd ever loved anything or anyone. 'I knew I loved you, wanted you and needed you, but there were reasons—stupid ones—why I thought we couldn't make a future together.'

He wouldn't mention her relationship with Harold. That was firmly in the past and could stay there, because Harold was dead. But he could tell her about the other reason, because it needed clearing up.

'The guy you live with. I've only spoken to him on the phone—the first time when I had to tell you of Harold's death, when he passed me over to you, and the second when he told me you'd gone out to the island. His tone alone told me he was defending his territory.'

Georgia lifted her head from where it rested against the warm angle of his shoulder, a slight, puzzled frown between her eyes as she looked at him. He brushed a tangle of hair back from her forehead and assured her, 'It's OK, sweetheart. I don't expect you to have lived the life of a nun for the past seven years. And from the way you respond to me I guess you can't be in a committed, serious relationship with him.'

She loved him for that, more than ever—if that were possible. Putting her hands on either side of his face, she drew his head down, kissing him until the breath left her body, and he said raggedly, against her mouth, 'We'll go back and move your things out. If he causes trouble, just leave him to me. You can stay at my London apartment until the wedding. Three weeks should give you enough time to buy a new hat! And then a long, long honeymoon. On the island? Would you like that?'

She threw her head back, her golden eyes dancing. 'Very much! I can't think of anywhere better.' Then she giggled irrepressibly, 'Oh, I do love you! You get the quaintest ideas! You don't have to defend me against an ex-lover's wrath—Ben isn't my lover, never was. He's simply a neighbour with aspirations in that direction. He tries it on and I slap him down. The number of jars of coffee he borrows would stock a supermarket, and I guess that when he answered the phone while I was on the island he was snooping.'

She sobered suddenly. The idea of Ben going into her apartment, probably pawing through her possessions, was horrible. 'There are only four apartments in the building, and all of us have spare keys to the others—a precaution in case of burst pipes and so on.'

'And he uses his to snoop around whenever you're out,' Jason said savagely. 'The first thing I'll do is make him hand it back. Not that it matters, because you'll be with me in London. We'll look for a proper home—a house in the country, darling?—when we're back from that extended honeymoon.'

'Jason.' She laid her finger over his lips to stop him. He was making so many plans her head was reeling. She shifted round on the luxurious leather upholstery so that she could face him more squarely.

'I won't be with you in London before the wedding.' She saw the sudden bleak flick of fear in his eyes and hurried on, because she couldn't bear him to think, if only for an instant, that she'd changed her mind. 'I need to work four weeks' notice; that means I have to stay where I am. I'll have to get in touch with my boss—Robin Ansley—in New York. He'll need to appoint my successor, and I'd like him and Kate, his wife, to be at our wedding. They couldn't have been kinder if they'd been my parents. And Sue and her American fiancé, and Guy, of course. So, if we marry in six weeks—'

'Four,' he stated. 'I can't wait a minute longer than that to put my ring on your finger.'

'Done!' she capitulated easily. She couldn't wait, either. The wedding arrangements would have to be done on the hoof, but that didn't matter. She could manage it. She could do anything as long as he loved her.

'And I,' he told her decisively, taking her hand and kissing the tips of her fingers, 'will stay with you at your apartment while you work out your notice. I'll have a meal waiting when you get home, and wash your smalls, and push your neighbour's teeth through the back of his head if he so much as shows his face!' He was smiling, but deadly serious. Never again would he put his work before her and her needs. 'That's if I can't persuade Ansley to waive your period of notice. I'll have a word with him when you phone, to let him know what's happening.'

Snuggling back into the warmth of his chest, she smiled a secret smile. He was taking charge, and for almost seven years no one, but no one, had been allowed that liberty. But she actually liked it. It made her feel secure, and totally loved for the first time in her life. And very, very feminine.

He slid his hands beneath her sweater, stroking the smooth line of her back, sliding them round to caress the sides of her aching breasts, sending her wild with longing, and said thickly, 'It's time we headed back to your place, your bed. Or, I'll start behaving like a randy teenager and ravish you in the back of the car!'

'Oh, goodness!' Georgia struggled up through the obliterating mists of rising passion. 'I'm due to meet the solicitor—' she shot a hasty look at her watch '—right now!'

'I'd forgotten about him,' Jason said, watching fondly as she tugged her clothing back in place, pushed her fingers through her glorious hair, trying to tame it. 'What's it about?'

'Some letter Mrs Moody found—and papers to sign for her and Baines' pensions.' She sounded breathless; she felt breathless, unbusinesslike. She would be late for the meeting. And she would *look* unbusinesslike, look as if she had just been thoroughly kissed. Which she had. She would look as if she was ecstatically happy. Which she most definitely was.

She grinned, because it didn't matter. 'So give me the keys and I'll get going.'

She held out her hand, and for a moment wondered if he would do no such thing, would insist on driving her there himself, leaving her beautiful car at the side of a ditch for someone to tow away and get rid of.

But slowly he took her keys from his pocket and put them in her outstretched hand, closing her fingers around them, and because she understood his reluctance—he'd been afraid that she'd drive herself into an accident, as Vivienne had, in what must have been a savagely reckless mood—she said, 'Thank you. I promise I'll drive carefully.'

'I'll hold you to that.' He smiled, but his voice was gruff as she opened the door and slid out. And by the time she'd started her engine the Jaguar was on the road, leading the way, the pace staid.

Georgia grinned. Give him time and he'd learn that she was a safe driver, could handle her powerful car, was always in control. She loved him, deeply and devotedly, always had and always would. But there were certain things...

There was only one safe passing place on the approach to Lytham.

Georgia flashed her headlights in warning and arrowed ahead, tucking back neatly to the side of the lane well before the next corner, and Jason sped up, laughing aloud.

The battle for mastery would never get serious. With Georgia, the provocative minx, it would always be fun.

CHAPTER THIRTEEN

THE drawing room at Lytham was overheated. Besides the central heating, Mrs Moody had provided them with a hearthful of blazing coals. Jason, sitting on the window seat, divorcing himself from the proceedings because whatever Georgia decided to do with her legacy was entirely down to her, ran a finger round the inside of the neck of his light sweater.

He had already disposed of his jacket, and still he felt stifled. He looked at Baines with a twinge of sympathy. The gardener was sitting close to the fire, and obviously wished he wasn't, but felt too out of his element to attempt to move. His face was red, his forehead beaded with sweat, and his thick fingers were plucking at the cloth cap he held on his heavy-corduroy-clad knees.

Mrs Moody stood just inside the door, looking as if she was wearing a steel corset, upright, stiff, her expression as dour as ever.

Only Georgia looked at ease, her graceful body bent over the papers the solicitor had asked her to sign, reading carefully, finally nodding and adding her signature.

'Thank you.' The solicitor slipped the signed papers back in his document case and named the generous sum that would be paid out each month—

enough to keep Mrs Moody in more than comfortable retirement and to make an adequate buffer for Baines, should the new owners of Lytham—whoever—not require his services.

Jason saw Baines go even redder with astonished pleasure, and caught the look of gratitude and relief Mrs Moody threw in Georgia's direction. For a moment or two he was swamped with self-loathing as he recalled the way he'd reacted to the new Georgia who had walked in here the day before Harold's funeral.

How he'd coldly informed her that as Harold hadn't remembered his loyal staff in his will she should put that right. She hadn't needed reminding; her generosity of spirit hadn't changed.

He had let past misunderstandings and bleak bitterness blind him to what she really was: his loving, generous darling.

Never, never again, he vowed vehemently. He would never, in all the years that lay ahead of them, cease to show her how much she was loved. She had had so very little of it up until now; he would make it up to her in spades.

'All that's left, at this time, is to hand you this letter.' The solicitor put a large white envelope on the table. 'The instructions are written in the late Mr Harcourt's hand.'

'I came across it in his shirt drawer,' Mrs Moody told Georgia, her tone more animated than Jason had ever heard it. Had she been worried about her future, where she would live when she got too old to work, how she would manage on the state pension?

'He was always so particular about his shirts. There was this drawer of new ones, still in Cellophane wrappers. I was gathering them up to send to a charity shop when I found it. I thought it might be important. Now, Miss Georgia, shall I bring in some tea?'

'Not for me, thank you,' the solicitor said, fastening the document case with fussy precision. 'I have another appointment waiting. I'm already late.'

And Baines, twisting his cap between his hands, mumbled his thanks to Georgia and followed the solicitor out, anxious to hurry back to his wife and tell her the good news.

Georgia said, 'I'd love some, Mrs Moody. We both would.'

As the housekeeper left the room Georgia picked up the envelope, her eyes puzzled. 'I wonder what this is?'

'Open it and see.' Jason hoped he didn't sound as edgy as he felt. Whatever private last messages that letter contained, he wasn't going to sit in judgement. He remembered her tears at Harold's funeral, her obvious sorrow, and wondered what they had meant to each other. He didn't want to know.

'Now why didn't I think of that?' She gave him a radiant smile and held out a hand to him. 'Let's read it together.'

Jason went, because when she called he always would, but crazily, considering the hot-house temperature of this room, he felt a trickle of ice run down his spine. A foreboding of what?

He stood at her side while she slit open the envelope but he made no attempt to read what was written on the two separate sheets of closely covered paper. He found he was holding his breath.

When she whispered his name, brushed her hair away from her face and looked up at him, he saw her cheeks were pale, wet with tears, and he gathered her to him, holding her. Because if she needed comfort—whatever the reason—he was here to give it her.

'You were—very fond of him.' He got the words out with difficulty. 'I saw how you wept at his funeral.' He ached for her to deny it, and knew she couldn't. Whatever Harold had said, in those last private words to her, it had left her weeping in his arms.

She said, 'Fond of Harold? In a way, I suppose.'

'You don't have to lie to me,' he told her, almost brusquely.

She lifted her head and shook it, biting down on her lower lip, grabbing her control back. 'I'm not lying. I did get to like him better after he came out to New York to tell me the news that Vivienne was dead and already buried.' She pulled a hankie out of her trouser pocket and blew her nose ferociously. 'He was so full of guilt—he couldn't stop apologising because he thought he'd ruined my life with those lies he'd told. I never did have the heart to tell him about the baby, and you wanting to marry me until you believed his lies. He was so full of remorse over putting the final nail in the coffin of my relationship with my mother that I couldn't heap anything more on him.'

'So you forgave him?' Jason tugged her back into his arms. He knew how different Harold had become after his wife's death: thoughtful, remorseful, shrinking in on himself.

'There didn't seem much point in harbouring old grudges,' she told him, her voice muffled by his sweater. 'He used to write, and sometimes I'd reply. Just odd snippets of news—he seemed lonely, and unhappy, and I felt more sorry for him than actually fond of him. I wasn't crying for him that day. The night before I'd dreamed of our baby—the first time in ages.'

'It still hurts you?' He could have punched his fist through a wall in frustration, but he held her gently, close to him. He wanted to fight every damn thing that hurt her, but was powerless, in this case, to do so.

'No, not since I knew you wanted our baby, too,' she told him, pulling away a little, her eyes glowing with love now. 'That little life was loved by both of us; that makes the difference. We can let it go—and there will be others. And before Mrs Moody comes back with that tea—' she held out the two sheets of paper '—read these. This one first.'

With a brief look at her, he took from her what appeared to be two separate letters, and scanned them quickly. One was from Vivienne, written to her daughter, and, as Georgia had indicated, he read that first.

The tone was jerky, almost hysterical, and told of her desire for a reconciliation, mentioned the unfinished letter she'd left behind on the island. Told of the way she couldn't blind herself any longer to Harold's furtive affairs. Of her shame and remorse at the way she'd made herself believe Harold's version of events when she'd walked in and found them wrapped around each other.

> If I'd believed you, I couldn't have gone on living with him. And I didn't want to lose what I'd got. So I told myself I believed him and washed my hands of you. I was a lousy mother, greedy and self-centred, and I have come to hate myself.

So that was why Georgia had shed those tears! Not speaking, he looped an arm around her waist and pulled her close, then read what Harold had written. Not much, just an apology and an explanation.

On his return to Lytham, after hearing of Vivienne's fatal accident, he'd found the letter she'd written among her things.

> I realised then what harm I'd done, to both of you. It changed me. But I still didn't have the courage to send the letter on to you. I give it to you now, and leave all I own to you. An attempt at recompense.

As he read, Georgia could see the relief on his face and she knew. She had always suspected that Jason believed she'd slept her way into her inheritance, that her relationship with her stepfather had been murky.

She took the sheets of paper from him, folded them and tucked them into her handbag, her face set. 'As I said before, you get the quaintest ideas.' She poked his flat midriff with her forefinger. 'You thought Harold was my sugar-daddy, and I let him be because I wanted his money. All of it.' She gave another jab. 'Admit it!'

He felt cold all over now, and at any moment he would start to shake. There was a tight knot in his chest and he couldn't breathe.

Was she about to tell him she couldn't marry, let alone love, a man who was capable of harbouring such hateful, demeaning thoughts? Walk out of his life again and leave him broken?

Unbelievably, though, her golden eyes were dancing now, and she was smiling. But he couldn't. He felt like a worm. 'I'm sorry, Georgia. So sorry.'

'Don't be.' She was actually grinning, and his heart began to beat again. 'You still wanted to marry me, even though you thought I was that dreadful. You must really love me, warts and all!'

And wasn't that the truth! He loved her more with each beat of his heart. She was wonderful, and he didn't deserve her, but he'd spend the rest of his life trying to!

His strong teeth gleamed whitely as he returned her smile. 'I really, truly do.' He picked her up and swung her round. 'But I am relieved to have finally got rid of those warts!'

'Tea,' Mrs Moody said from the doorway, and cleared her throat, smiling at their antics.

Jason put Georgia back on her feet, sliding her down his body. She looked flushed, radiant, utterly, utterly gorgeous. He lifted her hand to his mouth and kissed the backs of her fingers. 'Mrs Moody, very soon I'm going to frogmarch this little darling to the altar. Will you be the first to congratulate me?'

'And about time too, if you don't mind me saying it. I always knew you were right for each other,' the housekeeper said as Jason took the heavy tray from her and carried it to the table.

'Right.' He surveyed the silver teapot, the plates of thinly cut smoked salmon sandwiches, the rich fruitcake and the tiny sausage rolls. 'Make a start on this, both of you. I'm going to fetch some of Harold's champagne. I think the occasion demands it.'

Georgia poured the tea and handed a cup to Mrs Moody. 'Do sit down,' she said, and passed her the plate of sandwiches and saw her settled in the chair near the fire. She took her own tea to the sofa that flanked the table, so that Jason could sit beside her. 'Have you thought where you might live when this house is sold?'

'Well...' Mrs Moody put her teacup down on the delicate tripod table beside her. 'There's a cottage to let in the village. I've always fancied it—it's right next to the church. And with that generous pension—' her cheeks went pink with excitement '—I could easily afford it.'

'Then go for it!' Georgia nibbled at a triangular sandwich. 'I think I know the one you mean—it has a lovely front garden, full of flowers in the summer, and a rose arch over the gate?'

The older woman nodded vigorously, her mouth full of fruitcake, and Georgia wondered why she'd ever been frightened of her. 'See the estate agent first thing in the morning and take it,' she advised. 'Get in there before someone else does. And if you fancy anything from here—furnishings, bedlinen, china, anything—then do take what you want. Jason and I will have no use for it.'

They would find the right house for them, turn it into a real home, not a showplace, and there would be space for lots of children, and their pets, and it would be full of love and laughter.

'I can't tell you how grateful I am.' Mrs Moody had gone even more pink. 'But I'll tell you what I will do. I'll keep an eye on the folks who buy this place. You never know, it might turn out to be a happy home. It's the people, isn't it, who make a house happy?'

Georgia would have wholeheartedly agreed with that sentiment, but Jason walked in with two bottles of champagne and three glasses. The very best champagne, she noted. Harold had never stinted himself. Up until Vivienne's death he had indulged in every hedonistic pleasure that presented itself, but he had never known what it was like to be truly happy.

Neither had her mother.

Georgia said a silent goodbye to both of them and raised her foaming glass to Jason, to her future. And after they'd all toasted each other, and Mrs Moody had got decidedly giggly, Jason raised an eyebrow to Georgia.

'We could stay here tonight. What do you think?'

'Why not?' Why trail all the way back to Birmingham on a dark winter evening? She didn't mind where she was as long as she was with Jason. Lytham held no bad memories now, only good ones. 'If that's not too inconvenient for you?' she added to the housekeeper.

'Not a bit of it!' Mrs Moody sounded quite merry. 'Your room, sir? Or Miss Georgia's?'

'Mine,' Jason said decisively.

'Don't bother with an evening meal, Mrs Moody,' said Georgia. 'There's enough left here to feed a small army. So you might as well call it a day.'

As soon as they were alone, Jason joined her on the sofa. He'd kept his distance because, close to her, he wouldn't be able to keep his hands off her, and he hadn't wanted to embarrass the housekeeper.

'If we're not driving, I can open the other bottle,' he said, twining a long, lively strand of her hair through his fingers. 'Mrs Moody drank the lion's share.'

'Like water,' she agreed, fitting herself against his body, wrapping her arms around him. 'I hope she'll be all right, won't fall over her feet.'

'She'll be fine,' Jason murmured, lowering his

head and finding her soft, willing mouth. 'She's not incapable, falling-over drunk—just happy. You made her happy. You...' he parted her lips with the tip of his tongue '...make me happy.'

'I'm glad.' Momentarily she drew back, her hands touching his face. 'And I'm glad you said we'd use your room. It was where it all started, remember?'

'I've never forgotten.' His throat thickened. He'd tried to forget, but it hadn't been possible. No other woman had touched his heart as his darling did. No other woman had come near it.

'And it wasn't the start, not really,' he said, his voice thickening. 'Looking back, I think I began loving you for what you were long before that night, before I fell in love with you. And now—' he took her hands and laid them against his heart '—I think the time for talking's over, don't you?'

'I couldn't agree more!' Her smile was radiant, her eyes drowning with love as she wriggled close and slipped her hands beneath his sweater.

Four years later Georgia lay on Blue Rock's soft white sands and watched with drowsy eyes as Jason played with the twins at the water's edge. The little boys were three years old, with dark hair and golden eyes, sturdy bodies and decidedly independent minds.

She loved the three males in her life to pieces. Each year they came to their island in the sun and thoroughly enjoyed themselves. And every day in her busy, happy life just seemed to get better. She gave a contented little sigh and wriggled her bikini-clad body to get more comfy in the shade of the enormous umbrella. She'd put on weight, but, as Jason repeatedly assured her, in all the right places, so she didn't mind. He called her his Earth Mother, and she didn't mind that, either. She loved the big rambly home they'd found, loved cooking for him and the boys in the cosy farmhouse kitchen, turning the sprawling gardens into a paradise of flowers and vegetables. But, she thought, drifting into sleep on a wave of happiness, there was something missing...

She woke when Jason kissed her, and smiled for him, and she knew what it was—what was missing.

'I think it's time the boys had a new brother or sister. I'm feeling decidedly broody.'

'Is that a fact?' He eased his long, lithe body beside her. His skin was the colour of mahogany and her mouth went dry when she looked at him, the way it always did.

He reached up and tilted the umbrella, secluding them from the low cliffs, then slid his hands behind her, searching for the clasp that held the tiny bikini top in place.

Much as she wanted him to carry on, to strip her naked for his adoring eyes, she protested, 'Not in front of the twins—'

'Blossom whisked them away while you were sleeping, to give them a bath and their supper—I swear that woman gets bossier by the hour. So relax, honey-bunch, and I'll see what I can do to oblige.' He removed the scraps of fabric from her voluptuous body and grinned down at her. 'The things a guy has to do to keep his woman happy!'

MILLS & BOON®

Makes any time special

Enjoy a romantic novel from Mills & Boon®

Presents... *Enchanted* *Temptation*

Historical Romance *Medical Romance*

MILLS & BOON

Next Month's Romance Titles

Each month you can choose from a wide variety of romance novels from Mills & Boon®. Below are the new titles to look out for next month from the Presents...™ and Enchanted™ series.

Presents...™

A BOSS IN A MILLION	Helen Brooks
HAVING LEO'S CHILD	Emma Darcy
THE BABY DEAL	Alison Kelly
THE SEDUCTION BUSINESS	Charlotte Lamb
THE WEDDING-NIGHT AFFAIR	Miranda Lee
REFORM OF THE PLAYBOY	Mary Lyons
MORE THAN A MISTRESS	Sandra Marton
THE MARRIAGE EXPERIMENT	Catherine Spencer

Enchanted™

TYCOON FOR HIRE	Lucy Gordon
MARRYING MR RIGHT	Carolyn Greene
THE WEDDING COUNTDOWN	Barbara Hannay
THE BOSS AND THE PLAIN JAYNE BRIDE	Heather MacAllister
THE RELUCTANT GROOM	Emma Richmond
READY, SET...BABY	Christie Ridgway
THE ONE-WEEK MARRIAGE	Renee Roszel
UNDERCOVER BABY	Rebecca Winters

On sale from 3rd September 1999

H1 9908

Available at most branches of WH Smith, Tesco, Asda, Martins, Borders, Easons, Volume One/James Thin and most good paperback bookshops

MILLS & BOON

MEDICAL ROMANCE

HER PASSION FOR DR JONES by Lilian Darcy
Southshore - No.1 of 4

Dr Harry Jones is sure it's a mistake having Rebecca Irwin work in the practice. Despite the raging attraction between her and Harry, Rebecca fought her corner!

BACHELOR CURE by Marion Lennox
Bachelor Doctors

Dr Tessa Westcott burst into Mike Llewellyn's life like a red-headed whirlwind. She said exactly what she thought, and turned his ordered world upside down. It couldn't last. But Mike had to admit, she lightened his life.

HOLDING THE BABY by Laura MacDonald

Lewis's sister was abroad and he was left holding the baby—literally! He *badly* needed help with the three children and asked Jo Henry to be nanny. In a family situation, Jo and Lewis became *vividly* aware of each other...

SEVENTH DAUGHTER by Gill Sanderson

Specialist registrar Dr James Owen was everything Dr Delyth Price ever wanted in a man. But Delyth had a gift not everyone understood. James seemed prepared to listen, if not to believe. Then she discovered his lighthearted side, and fell even deeper into love...

Available from 3rd September 1999

Available at most branches of WH Smith, Tesco, Asda, Martins, Borders, Easons, Volume One/James Thin and most good paperback bookshops

Spoil yourself next month
with these four novels from

TEMPTATION

MACKENZIE'S WOMAN by JoAnn Ross

Bachelor Auction

Kate Campbell had to persuade Alec Mackenzie to take part in a charity bachelor auction. This rugged adventurer would have women bidding millions for an hour of his time. Trouble was, Alec wasn't really a bachelor. Though nobody knew it—he was married to Kate!

A PRIVATE EYEFUL by Ruth Jean Dale

Hero for Hire

Nick Charles was a bodyguard on a vital assignment. But no one had yet told him exactly what that assignment was! So he was hanging around a luxury resort, waiting... Then along came luscious Cory Leblanc and Nick just knew she was a prime candidate—for *something*...

PRIVATE LESSONS by Julie Elizabeth Leto

Blaze

'Harley' turned up on Grant Riordan's doorstep and sent his libido skyrocketing. Hired as the 'entertainment' for a bachelor party, she was dressed like an exotic dancer but had the eyes of an innocent. Unfortunately, after a little accident, she didn't have a clue who she was...

SEDUCING SYDNEY by Kathy Marks

Plain-Jane Sydney Stone was feeling seriously out of place in a glamorous Las Vegas hotel, when she received a mysterious note arranging a date—for that night! She was sure the message must have been delivered to the wrong woman. But maybe she'd just go and find out...

Our hottest **TEMPTATION** authors bring you...

Blaze

Three sizzling love stories available in one volume in September 1999.

Midnight Heat
JoAnn Ross

A Lark in the Dark
Heather MacAllister

Night Fire
Elda Minger

MILLS & BOON®

London streets aren't just paved with gold—they're home to three of the world's most eligible bachelors!

NOTTING HILL GROOMS

Presents…™ authors bring you the **Notting Hill Grooms**—eligible bachelors each looking for a wife.

MARY LYONS
Reform of the Playboy
published September 1999

SOPHIE WESTON
The Millionaire Affair
published October 1999

Available at most branches of WH Smith, Tesco, Asda, Martins, Borders, Easons, Volume One/James Thin and most good paperback bookshops

FREE!
4 Books
and a surprise gift!

We would like to take this opportunity to thank you for reading this Mills & Boon® book by offering you the chance to take FOUR more specially selected titles from the Presents...™ series absolutely FREE! We're also making this offer to introduce you to the benefits of the Reader Service™—

- ★ FREE home delivery
- ★ FREE gifts and competitions
- ★ FREE monthly Newsletter
- ★ Books available before they're in the shops
- ★ Exclusive Reader Service discounts

Accepting these FREE books and gift places you under no obligation to buy; you may cancel at any time, even after receiving your free shipment. Simply complete your details below and return the entire page to the address below. *You don't even need a stamp!*

YES! Please send me 4 free Presents...™ books and a surprise gift. I understand that unless you hear from me, I will receive 6 superb new titles every month for just £2.40 each, postage and packing free. I am under no obligation to purchase any books and may cancel my subscription at any time. The free books and gift will be mine to keep in any case.

P9EB

Ms/Mrs/Miss/Mr ....Initials................................
BLOCK CAPITALS PLEASE

Surname..

Address..

....

....Postcode ....

Send this whole page to:
THE READER SERVICE, FREEPOST CN81, CROYDON, CR9 3WZ
(Eire readers please send coupon to: P.O. BOX 4546, KILCOCK, COUNTY KILDARE)

Offer not valid to current Reader Service subscribers to this series. We reserve the right to refuse an application and applicants must be aged 18 years or over. Only one application per household. Terms and prices subject to change without notice. Offer expires 29th February 2000. As a result of this application, you may receive further offers from Harlequin Mills & Boon and other carefully selected companies. If you would prefer not to share in this opportunity please write to The Data Manager at the address above.

Mills & Boon is a registered trademark owned by Harlequin Mills & Boon Limited.
Presents... is being used as a trademark.

THE Regency COLLECTION
Where rogues find romance

Look out for the fifth volume in this limited collection of Regency Romances from Mills & Boon® in September.

Featuring:

My Lady Love
by Paula Marshall

and

Four in Hand
by Stephanie Laurens

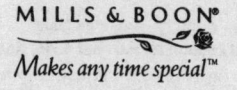

Still only £4.99

MILLS & BOON®
Makes any time special™

Available at most branches of WH Smith, Tesco, Martins, Borders, Easons, Volume One/James Thin and most good paperback bookshops